Subhadra Sen Gupta has written over forty books for children because she thinks children are the best readers in the world. She loves telling stories woven around history; plotting complicated mysteries and crazy adventures; dreaming up ghostly tales and scripting comic books. In 2014 she was awarded the Bal Sahitya Puraskar by the Sahitya Akademi for her children's books. If you want to start a conversation with her, send her an email here and she promises to reply: subhadrasg@gmail.com.

Other titles in the series

The Teenage Diary of
Jahanara

Subhadra Sen Gupta

talking
CUB

An Imprint of Speaking Tiger

TALKING CUB
Published by Speaking Tiger Publishing Pvt. Ltd
4381/4 Ansari Road, Daryaganj, New Delhi–110002, India

First published by Scholastic India (Private) Limited
in 2001
This edition published in Talking Cub by Speaking Tiger
in paperback in 2019

ISBN: 978-93-88874-14-4
eISBN: 978-93-88874-13-7

10 9 8 7 6 5 4 3 2 1

Typeset in Goudy Old Style by Jojy Philip

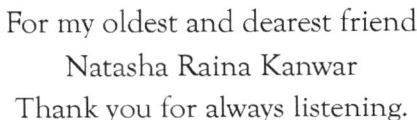

For my oldest and dearest friend
Natasha Raina Kanwar
Thank you for always listening.

The Teenage Diary of Jahanara

The Twenty-First Year of the Reign of His Majesty Nuruddin Jahangir
Mandu, 1626

Spring in Mandu

THE SUN WAS SETTING WHEN Dara and I saw the rising ball of dust, far away where the road curved. We were standing on the highest terrace of the Jahaz Mahal Palace and from there we had spied the horseman racing towards the royal camp.

Dara turned to me and said, 'The messenger won't arrive tonight. It is getting dark and they must have set up camp by now. So, maybe it will be sometime tomorrow.'

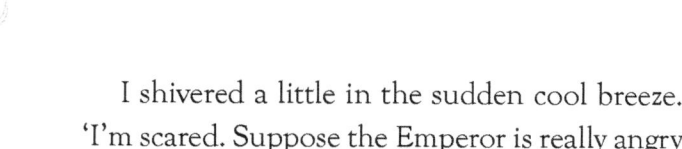

I shivered a little in the sudden cool breeze. 'I'm scared. Suppose the Emperor is really angry with Father? We could be in trouble, Dara!'

Even cheerful Dara looked a bit solemn. 'We'll only know tomorrow when Father reads the royal order.'

We watched the horseman spring down and run to the part of the palace where Father was at work. The rider was one of the soldiers stationed as a lookout on the road that led to the north. His job was to inform my father the moment he saw the royal entourage sent by Emperor Jahangir from Agra. Now we knew that the royal messenger carrying the royal order or the farman was not far away.

I am certain something important is going to happen tomorrow and I want to write it all down. Dara laughs at me and says I am writing a diary because I fancy myself as a writer, but that is not really true. What I love is the act of writing itself, to dip my pen into the ink and then draw the words on paper and see them shine like black jewels on the cream pages. Drawing out the curves and the dots, the sharp downward

lines, our script is at times like a painting. I think words are the most beautiful thing on earth.

Maybe, Dara is right and I am wasting my time; but I, Jahanara, a Mughal princess, want to keep a record of everything that happens in my life. I need these pages where I can express my innermost thoughts, my dreams, my hopes and fears. I must find a place to hide these pages from my sister Roshanara's prying eyes. She would tease me mercilessly if she read what I have written. Her teasing hurts; she is not kind and gentle like Dara.

Nearly midnight

I waited till everyone was asleep and then taking one of the thickest candles from the sitting room I found this quiet corner of the palace balcony to write. The soft night breeze is making the thin curtains on the doors sway and the candle flame flicker.

Just because I am only twelve years old, everyone thinks I don't understand things. I understand much more than my eleven-year-old brother Dara does. He is such a dreamer,

he doesn't even notice what is happening right before his eyes. If Dara is reading, listening to poetry or to one of the court singers, he wouldn't even turn his head even if my father were to ride out to war.

Shah Jahan is my father, a prince of the royal family of the Timurids. The people call us the dynasty of the Mughals because one of our ancestors was the Mongol conqueror Chengiz Khan. We, however, prefer to call ourselves Timurids because we also trace our family tree to the great Persian king Timur. My father says we like our connection to the cultured Persians with their palaces, mosques, art and literature but we are not that proud of the horse riding, nomadic Mongols who lived in tents and cooked their food on open fires.

Anyway, my father is the third son of the Mughal Emperor Jahangir, the Shahenshah of Hindustan. My mother, Arjamand Bano Begum, is one of my father's three wives and, fortunately for us, his favourite one. He likes to keep her by his side and Mother always travels with him, even when he goes to war.

For the last five years Father has been at war with the Emperor. He had a disagreement with the Empress, Nur Jahan Begum, who is Father's stepmother, and then declared war. He has been fighting the imperial forces since then. As he wandered all over the kingdom, Mother has always been with him. And so have we, their six children—I, Jahanara, my four brothers Dara Shikoh, Muhammad Shuja, Aurangzeb and Murad Baksh and my only sister Roshanara.

The funny thing is that I never thought this would happen to us. When we were living in Agra, I could never have imagined that Father and Grandfather could be fighting each other and we would be chased by the imperial army like a bunch of robbers. How can I forget that it was my father who was the favourite son of Jahangir? He was the son the Emperor trusted, listened to and consulted on important matters of the state.

During those happy days at Agra, with Father so busy with the work of the kingdom, everyone took it for granted that Shah Jahan was the heir apparent and would one day become king. How

did it all go so wrong and so fast? Was it the fault of the Empress Nur Jahan as everyone says? Or did Father make a mistake? I wish I knew.

And now the royal messenger is coming to our palace with a farman from the emperor and my heart sinks like the fading light from this guttering candle. The order decides our fate and somehow I know, the news will not be good...

The next Day

It is very early, and I thought I would write a little before everyone woke up. This diary is becoming my favourite occupation and all day I long to sit down and write in it. It is like having a very private, whispered conversation with your best friend, someone who will never betray your confidence. There are so many curious eyes and ears in the harem that I can only trust a diary with my thoughts.

I looked up and stared out into the garden of the palace, at the borders filled with blooming flowers—roses, lilies and jasmines—whose perfume drifts up to this upper balcony where I sit. I love this palace with its carved stone walls, gardens, shady trees and pretty pools covered with lotus flowers floating on their dark green plate-like leaves.

A moment ago, I saw a kingfisher fly down and dive into the water, its turquoise feathers glittering like jewels in the rays of the early morning sun. There is a bulbul singing in the tree, somewhere. I wish I could stay here forever and never have to travel anymore. I am so tired of wandering...

Enough of dreaming, let me get back to the story I began last night. I fell asleep while writing and my mother's companion Sati-un-nissa Khanum found me there, still holding the pen and with my face resting on the paper. She said I looked like one of the sleeping clerks in the palace office who always doze off over their account book when the officers are not looking.

Sati-un-nissa finds something amusing in everything she sees and she is very good at cheering Mother when she is not feeling well. My mother had ten children in the fourteen years she has been married and six of us have survived. So she often feels tired and at times is

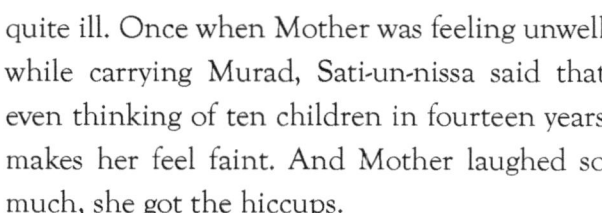

quite ill. Once when Mother was feeling unwell while carrying Murad, Sati-un-nissa said that even thinking of ten children in fourteen years makes her feel faint. And Mother laughed so much, she got the hiccups.

Our life was so different five years ago when we lived happily in Agra. Father was busy helping the Emperor. Even though he had four sons, Jahangir only trusted my father with the important work. His other sons were Khusro, Pervez and Shahriyar. Father was first called Khurram and then given the title of Shah Jahan after he had led a successful campaign to the Deccan in the south.

Khusro, Pervez and Shahriyar are all my father's half-brothers, born of different queens. In the Mughal household, half-brothers are often brought up separately and my father is not close to his half-brothers. The eldest son, my uncle Khusro, was born to the princess of Amber, Man Bai, while my father was born to the Jodhpur princess, Jagat Gosain. Both these princesses came from Hindu royal families. Since the time of my great-grandfather Akbar,

the Mughal men often marry into Hindu royal families and as a matter of fact both my great-grandmother and grandmother are Hindus.

I think a lot about our life in Agra. We all stayed in the palaces inside the huge fort built by Emperor Akbar. I, of course, grew up in the harem called the Mahal, where all the royal women stayed in seclusion, hidden from the eyes of the world, behind purdah. The Mahal has many palaces and broad corridors with rooms on both sides. All the queens and princesses have their own apartments. We stayed with Mother who had her own set of four rooms, her own maids and, of course, the company of Sati-un-nissa.

The Mahal area is closed off from the rest of the palace by huge doors and Rajput soldiers stand on guard outside. Only men of the royal family are allowed inside and a few others like Asaf Khan, who is my mother's father and a senior minister.

Inside the Mahal is a world of women—princesses, queens, concubines, maids, cooks, gardeners, washerwomen, even female singers,

dancers and painters. Around them wander the slaves who keep a close eye on everything and report regularly to the king.

Some of the women have been married from royal families. Others have been brought into the harem on the whim of a prince, who found them beautiful. Many have been born behind the walls of the Mahal. Some women say that once you entered the harem, no one saw your face again. You disappeared like a bejeweled ghost and after a few years, even your own family forgot you existed.

It is much easier here in Mandu and the discipline in the women's quarters is quite easy. Here you don't have soldiers at every door and at times even Mother goes out on walks and rides in the carriage, properly veiled. And Dara and I do wander about the palace and gardens quite often; no one scolds us as long as we do not try to go outside the fortress gates.

I hear the others waking...I better put these pages away...

Afternoon

The royal messenger has not arrived so far. It seems the soldier we saw yesterday evening had been stationed three days' ride from here and he had seen the royal entourage from the top of a hill, far away down the road. Father told Mother that it would be at least five days before they arrive. So we all have to be patient and wait.

Father came to our rooms for lunch. The royal men usually eat in the harem unless there is some special banquet. As it is not so formal here as in Agra, if Father is not delayed by work, we children also eat with him. When the drums announced noon, Mother and Sati-un-nissa bustled about instructing the maids to set out the food. First the carpet in the living room was brushed, then the dining cloth was laid on it with the bowls, plates, and glasses.

Once Father arrives the food will be brought from the kitchen by the maids. Every dish is tasted at the kitchen door to make sure it is not poisoned and then sealed by the chef. The Mughal princes have many enemies and they have to be very careful. Our food taster is paid well

for putting his life at risk. Sati-un-nissa says that the man gets paid to eat from the royal kitchen everyday, so he shouldn't really complain.

It was an hour past noon when Father arrived. He picked up my youngest brother Murad who is six and sat down to ask us what we did all day. Dara and I sat close to him and talked at the same time. We had so many questions for him.

'Abbu, Jahanara and I saw a horseman last evening.'

'Did he bring any news about the royal messenger?'

He gave us a surprised glance. 'How did you two see him? He had come in through the soldier's gate and that is round the corner from here.'

'We were on the roof.'

'On the roof? Just the two of you?'

'Well, Abbu,' I stroked his arm trying to calm him down. 'We were careful not to go the edge. We are old enough, we won't fall.'

'You didn't answer my question about the horseman.' Dara was not going to give up till Father told us everything.

'I will tell you after lunch. I'm hungry.' Father got up to go and sit down for lunch. Mother waved at the maids who came in carrying the food.

I love it when the whole family eats together, though Mother and Sati-un-nissa have a hard time keeping us children well behaved. Dara and I quickly went and sat on either side of Father, Shuja and Aurangzeb sat with Mother, Murad was being fed by a maid.

The moment Roshanara realized she couldn't sit next to either Mother or Father, she threw a tantrum. So Father made me move so that she could sit next to him. My sister is such a troublesome girl; always complaining about me and nothing ever makes her happy. She is convinced that Father loves Dara and me more than her. But then, if she is going to be so nasty and complaining all the time, who can love her? Mother says that if she moans too often her pretty face will turn into that of a witch. And I know she spies on us and then carries tales to Mother.

Aurangzeb, who is eight, sat next to me and I served him some of the fragrant biryani, the spicy rice with delicious pieces of meat, flavoured with saffron. Next to Dara, he is my favourite brother. Shuja is very naughty and spends his days with the other boys and loves to wrestle and ride horses. Murad is, of course, much too small.

Aurangzeb often drifts around me in his silent way, his large eyes following everything. He doesn't say much but at times I think he notices things much more than Dara. He can ask the strangest questions and he did so now as he thoughtfully chewed at a bone.

'Abbu, can you disobey a royal order?'

We all stopped eating to turn and stare at him. Finding all our eyes on him, he ducked his head shyly and added, 'I mean, you are at war with Grandfather Jahangir, aren't you, Abbu?'

Father just gave an impatient snort and went on eating. I've noticed, he is often a bit irritated by Aurangzeb's questions. When it comes to Dara and me, we can ask him anything.

Mother sighed and said, 'Aurangzeb, can your Father at least eat his lunch in peace? I don't want any more silly questions over food.'

Aurangzeb was silent, his head was bent but I knew he would ask the question again. He never forgets anything and he never gives up. Once he badgered Dara and me for a whole week till we taught him to play chess and within a few days, he was beating both of us. Aurangzeb always gets what he wants.

So I wasn't surprised at all when over the dessert of creamy kheer he said quietly to Father, 'Abbu, what will you do if the royal order asks you to surrender? Will you be made a prisoner?'

'That's it.' Father put down his spoon. 'All of you to the next room.' He washed his hands in the silver water bowls, wiped them on the towel held out by a maid and marched out. Saying over his shoulders, 'I don't have children, I have little politicians. Come along now.'

'But I haven't finished my kheer!' Shuja wailed. My fat brother really loves eating. 'I'm not going. I didn't bother Abbu with silly questions.'

Mother said, 'I am not going either. I want to finish my lunch.'

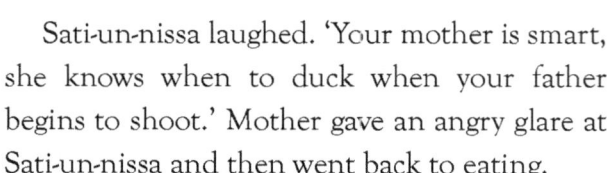

Sati-un-nissa laughed. 'Your mother is smart, she knows when to duck when your father begins to shoot.' Mother gave an angry glare at Sati-un-nissa and then went back to eating.

Giving a last look at my half-eaten bowl of kheer, I got up. When Father said 'Now!' in that tone of voice, you listened and moved fast. Roshanara didn't want to miss anything and tried to gobble up as much as she could and nearly choked, making Dara laugh.

As she ushered us out of the room Sati-un-nissa whispered, 'You four listen quietly to him. Do not interrupt, no arguments and no more questions!' The last order was aimed at Aurangzeb, who grinned, quite unrepentant.

So it was just the four of us—Dara, Aurangzeb, Roshanara and I who straggled into the bedroom where Father sat leaning against a bolster, chewing a paan. I sneaked a quick look at his face and saw the frown across his broad brow and my heart sank.

'Sit down,' he said. 'Today I'll answer all your questions but after that, I don't want to hear anything from you four again. Is that clear?'

'I didn't ask you anything, Abbu!' Roshanara was looking very saintly, 'I would never disturb your lunch, you know that.'

'Do I? Your tantrum disturbs me quite a lot.'

'I'll make them behave, Abbu,' I said. 'I'm the eldest and I'll make sure.'

Father smiled and pulled me closer and I leaned against him as the others crowded around. That is one good thing about Father, he never stays angry with us for long.

Actually, Father is very different from the other Mughal princes. Usually, the Mughal men are not too interested in their children and only notice the sons when they grow up. The children grow up in the Mahal with their mothers and are taken on formal visits to their fathers. Our Father likes to have his family with him. Sati-un-nissa says we get away with a lot because he is so easy-going. If my grandfather Jahangir had been so rude to his father Akbar, he would have been locked in his rooms for a week and put on a vegetarian diet.

Father looked at Dara. 'Yes, you are right. The royal messenger is on his way but he is

at least five days away. My soldier rode fast, changing horses along the way and so he came faster. The royal entourage moves slowly, you know that.'

'So we have to wait.' Dara gave an impatient sigh.

'That's right. Royal children need to learn some patience!' said Father firmly.

'Will he bring bad news, Abbu?' I asked anxiously.

He smiled down at me and said, 'I don't think so, Jahan. You must remember something. I am no longer at war with His Majesty, our King Jahangir. I sued for peace if you remember, Aurangzeb?'

'Yes, Abbu.' Aurangzeb nodded thoughtfully. 'But you have been at war for four years and your army has fought the imperial forces many times.'

'Yes. There has been a disagreement between His Majesty and me. But don't forget, he is both my father and my king. A farman is a royal order and it is being sent by my father, so I could not possibly disobey it.'

Aurangzeb looked up. 'He was also the father of Uncle Khusro and he gave the order to blind him.'

Father reached out to touch Aurangzeb's head, making my brother smile. 'So that is what is bothering you! Stop worrying like that. Khusro was forgiven many times and he was punished only when he would not stop rebelling against our father. I am not doing that. I have sued for peace and ended the war.'

I thought of Prince Khusro and shivered. Sometimes I think his unhappy ghost will haunt the House of the Mughals forever.

Friday morning

Today is Jumma, the day of prayers, and we all went to the mosque in the morning. Dara, Shuja and Aurangzeb joined Father and the other men in the open courtyard, while Roshanara and I prayed with Mother and Sati-un-nissa behind the reed curtains.

I knew that every member of the family prayed very hard and my prayers were simple. 'Please Allah, keep my family safe. May the Emperor

forgive Father and not punish him. And please, please Allah, I want to go back to Agra!'

Afternoon

Father was very quiet all morning and he has been closeted with Mother in the bedroom since right after lunch. I wonder what they are discussing for so long. Must be the problem of the royal messenger.

Dara, Shuja and Aurangzeb have all gone out riding and I have the corner of the balcony to myself. Sati-un-nissa is sitting at the other end teaching Roshanara to embroider a veil, so I can write in peace.

There is the curtained doorway of Mother's bedroom behind me and sometimes I can hear snatches of their conversation and the name that I hear most often is of the Empress Nur Jahan. At times Father calls her 'Our Saintly Malika Nur Jahan Begum' in a very sarcastic manner and it makes Mother laugh.

What is so sad is that just a few years ago all of them—my parents and Nur Jahan were such good friends.

I must admit, I find the Empress Nur Jahan quite fascinating. She is my grandfather Jahangir's last and youngest wife. He married her quite late in his life, when he was forty-two and by then all his four sons were grown-up men. My father was already a young man of nineteen and a prince busy with the work of the kingdom. Nur Jahan herself was thirty-four, a widow with a young daughter. She was the daughter of Jahangir's minister Itimad-ud-daula. After her first husband died, she entered the Mahal as a companion to one of the senior queens of Emperor Akbar named Ruqaiyya Begum. Jahangir saw her and decided to marry her.

In the beginning no one took it all very seriously, after all, kings are allowed to marry as many women as they want. Nur Jahan was very beautiful and everyone thought she was just another passing fancy of the king. Within a few months they realized that this marriage was different.

Nur Jahan was no ordinary young queen. She became her husband's greatest confidant and Jahangir did nothing without consulting her.

Every royal order was sent to her to read and she kept the royal seal and put the seal only on the orders she approved of. My grandfather trusted her completely. If Nur Jahan recommended someone for the job of a governor or army commander, Jahangir immediately agreed. If any nobleman was foolish enough to displease her in any way, his career in the royal service was over.

A year after her marriage, Nur Jahan arranged another wedding. This was of her niece Arjamand Bano Begum with Jahangir's third son, Prince Khurram-Shah Jahan. That is right, Nur Jahan is my mother's aunt. My grandfather Asaf Khan and she are brother and sister. They are the children of Minister Itimad-ud-daula, my great-grandfather.

So suddenly two daughters of Itimad-ud-daula's family were married into the Mughal clan. One became a queen; the other was now a princess.

In the years at Agra while I was growing up, all of them worked together like one family. There was my grandfather Jahangir and his beloved queen Nur Jahan. Then the senior minister

Asaf Khan, who was also my grandfather. And with them my father Shah Jahan and his wife Arjamand Bano. So my mother also became quite an influential lady.

In those days in Agra, while I wandered about the Mahal, I would hear the women talk about how powerful Nur Jahan had become. How it was she who really ran the empire! It always made me wonder how a woman who lived behind the doors of the Mahal could run the empire. She could not sit in the court of the Diwan-i-Aam and listen to the petitioners and the requests from the subjects or judge the legal cases like the Emperor. She couldn't consult ministers and ambassadors in the Diwan-i-Khas. How did she run the empire?

Whenever we went to visit her, she was like any other woman in the family. She would give us gifts of clothes and toys and feed us sweets. She behaved more like an indulgent grandaunt and not the most powerful woman in the kingdom, as the Mahal women called her.

The Empress is the most stunningly beautiful woman I have ever seen; and remember, the

Mughal harem has many beautiful women. Sometimes when she was all dressed up for a banquet, it was difficult to take eyes off her face. Mother is very beautiful too, but Nur Jahan Begum has something so dazzling about her that whenever I was near her I would just sit and watch her every move.

She is very fair, after all, they are of Persian blood. The pupils of her large, shining eyes under the arched brows are not black but a shade of dark grey. She has a sharp, straight nose and pink, curving lips. She is quite tall and slim and walks straight, with quick steps, like a dancer.

Mother is beautiful in a much softer way. Her cheeks are rounder, her lips curve gently and her eyes always smile. Mother is easy to love. We all found Nur Jahan a little scary. Dara and I always behaved carefully around her. When she looked down at me with a frown, I felt she could read all my thoughts.

But she was always very kind to us. She remembered that Dara liked to read and got him rare books. And she threw these magnificent

banquets on the birthday of the Emperor with a feast of exotic dishes as well as dancers and musicians.

I have to stop now. Father just left and Mother has come out into the balcony and shot a curious glance at my papers. I don't want her to read what I have written. Mother can be very strange when it comes to her family and the Empress is her aunt after all. I don't think she and Father will approve of my writing about her in a diary.

Later that night

All day my head has been full of thoughts about Nur Jahan Begum. I suppose it is because we all know that the farman may carry the signature of Jahangir but it would have been dictated by her.

If the Empress decides to punish my father, I believe Grandfather Jahangir would do little to stop her. We hear he is very ill and is often not interested in the work of the kingdom. And it is she who issues the royal orders.

Tonight, I have found another quiet place where I can write—Sati-un-nissa's room, at her

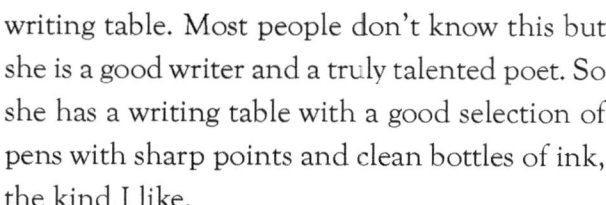

writing table. Most people don't know this but she is a good writer and a truly talented poet. So she has a writing table with a good selection of pens with sharp points and clean bottles of ink, the kind I like.

Sati-un-nissa's days are all so busy taking care of Mother, who is often very tired and wants to lie down, that she gets very little time to write. So it is often late at night that she lights a candle and sits here, and she says, she 'weaves her dreams on paper with the thread of her black ink.' I like that phrase because I am doing my own weaving with words now. It is only Sati-un-nissa who really understands my need to write.

Tonight when I came out after dinner, I found cold breeze blowing and it looked like it would rain. I wondered if I should sit in the balcony. She saw my face and said, 'Use my writing table. It is cold and windy outside.'

'What about you, Khanum Jaan? Won't you be writing?'

'Not tonight. I have just received some poems from Ajmer, I want to read them.' Then she touched my head, running her fingers

through my hair, 'And what were you writing all afternoon?'

'I was remembering the Empress.'

'Ah! Yes. Everyone is thinking of her today.'

So now I continue with my memories of Agra and of Nur Jahan—of Dara and I learning how she ran the kingdom from behind the veil of the harem.

We left Agra when I was eight. Just a few months before, Dara and I became really curious about Nur Jahan. It all began when Nur Jahan arranged the marriage of her daughter Ladili Begum with Prince Shahriyar. Ladili Begum is her daughter from her first marriage. Shahriyar is Jahangir's youngest son and my father's half-brother. So Nur Jahan was once again arranging a dynastic match.

Suddenly, we began to hear whispers about how Nur Jahan no longer favoured Father and was making Shahriyar the king's favourite. So far everyone thought Father was the heir apparent. Now the rumours were that Nur Jahan wanted Shahriyar to be chosen instead so that her daughter Ladili could become the next queen.

One morning, Dara and I wandered up to the palace where the Empress stayed. The slave guarding the door gave us a suspicious stare and asked, 'Have the Prince and Princess been invited by the Malika Begum to visit her?'

Slaves can be so rude and curious. Some of them behave like they are royalty themselves and the one called Dildar, who guards Nur Jahan's door, is by far the worst. So we expected to be questioned and Dara and I knew our answer.

I showed him the two books I was carrying and said, 'Malika Begum had given us these books to read. We have finished reading them and would like to return them to her library.'

'You could have sent them by the hands of a maid, there was no need for you two to carry these heavy books yourself.'

'Now that we have brought them,' Dara was doing his best to act very royal and superior, 'may we go in and return them to the bookshelves?'

'There is no need, my little prince.' Dildar bent a smiling face, his dark fleshy cheeks coming close to me, making me flinch. 'Give

them to me, Princess Jahanara, I'll put them back.' And he held out his hand.

As Dara and I were wondering what to do next, one of Nur Jahan's maids stuck her head out of the door and asked: 'Who is at the door, Dildar? The Malika heard you talking to someone.'

'Prince Dara and Princess Jahanara are here. They want to return some books.'

'Let them in.'

Dara and I grinned in triumph at Dildar, who was politely bowing us in, and went inside. The maid had come down to greet us. She took the books from me and said, 'The Malika Begum would like to meet you two. Go right in, she is in the living room.'

'Is His Majesty, our grandfather, also here?' I asked.

I liked meeting Grandfather. When he was in a good mood, he made me laugh.

The maid shook her head. 'Malika Begum is alone and very busy with her work, so don't be too noisy.'

The Empress was sitting, leaning against

a bolster and looked up to smile at us. She sat surrounded by rolls of paper that she was reading. By her side stood an ink stand and at times she was making notes on the papers. Next to her, the royal seal was kept on a small wooden stand. The seal was like a large ring with a round head with carvings on it and had an ebony handle. The face of the seal was about double the size of a coin.

I knew these yellow parchment rolls contained royal orders. Father read them too when he worked in Mother's room. I had read a few; they were all about the taxes from the provinces and the mustering of soldiers for the imperial army.

Dara and I bowed to Nur Jahan and I thanked her formally for the books. She waved to us to sit down on the carpet near her and asked, 'Which one did you like the most? The poetry of Faizi or the stories of Harun al Rashid?'

I was surprised she remembered the names of the books she had given us.

'I liked the stories of Harun al Rashid,' said Dara.

I frowned trying to answer her. 'I like reading poetry but I don't always understand it.'

Nur Jahan picked up the royal seal and dipping it into red ink she stamped one of the rolls of paper. This meant that this official order now had the approval of the Emperor.

'You are a bit young for that poetry, I suppose. In a few years you will enjoy it more.' She reached out to take another roll of parchment.

'You will read all these papers now?' I asked curiously. 'There are so many of them.'

'I read them every day. Otherwise how will I know if the kingdom is being run properly? His Majesty expects me to read everything carefully and tell him if I find anything wrong.'

Dara and I leaned forward eagerly.

'What could go wrong?' Dara wanted to know.

She gave us a quick glance. 'Well, it is time one learnt a little about how the empire is run.' She opened out one roll. 'Take this one. It is a report from our governor in Bengal. He says that there is a famine in the Parganas and he has not been able to collect the revenue from the farmers.'

Dara and I were still looking very puzzled.

'What is wrong with that?' I asked.

Nur Jahan picked up another roll and said, 'This is a report from one of our spies in Bengal and he says that the governor plans to keep back some of the taxes that he has collected by giving the excuse of the famine. This spy has visited the Parganas and he has been told that the governor has collected the full tax even though the farmers said their crops had failed.'

'You have spies?' I asked surprised.

'We have spies everywhere. Otherwise how will we know what is really happening in the empire? This is a very big kingdom, remember. The spies come and personally report to His Majesty every day.'

'So what will you do?' asked Dara.

'Are you going to punish the governor?'

'In a way. His Majesty will send an order saying that the farmers in the Parganas are to be given help from the taxes collected in Bengal. And I will send an officer with the order and this officer will check all the tax accounts and make sure the orders are carried out.'

The Empress had asked one of the maids to get us something to eat and now plates of sweets, salty fries, and glasses of sherbet arrived. She also picked up a glass of sherbet and sipping it went on working. Then Dara, never able to keep his mouth shut, blurted out, 'Malika Begum, are you the most powerful woman in the Mughal Empire?'

I swallowed nervously as Nur Jahan turned to look at Dara. For a moment she looked thoughtfully at us and then her lips curved slightly in an amused smile. 'Now, where did you hear that?'

'The women in the Mahal say so.'

She leaned back against the bolster and said, 'The most powerful person in the empire is your grandfather. I just help him. Whatever happens in the empire is the way he wishes and I can do nothing without his permission. I am like a minister who makes his burdens a little lighter.'

'But can a woman be a minister and help run a kingdom?' I asked curiously. 'We are not allowed to go out of the Mahal.'

'You can do a lot from inside the Mahal. You just have to know how. I meet officials and noblemen and listen to their reports.'

Dara and I were so surprised we just looked at her.

She laughed. 'When His Majesty meets these men I sit behind a curtain and listen to them and if I think it necessary I ask questions. Also there is my brother Asaf Khan, your grandfather.'

We nodded.

'My brother tells me what is happening outside and we discuss matters and decide what needs to be done.'

Then she said something that I will always remember, 'I may not sit on the throne in the Diwan-i-Aam but I know everything that is happening in this kingdom of Jahangir.'

There was something in the way she looked at me when she said this that made me very uncomfortable. What did she think? That Dara and I were also like her spies? That we would report everything to Father? I do not know why but there is very little trust within our family.

The Mughals love their brothers and sons but they never trust them.

Ow! My fingers are stiff and aching and my eyes are heavy with sleep. Goodnight, my dear Diary!

Two days after Jumma

Father was called away very early. When we saw Father go out, Dara and I followed him at a distance, out to the courtyard. We saw a dusty soldier spring down from his horse and run and bow to Father. The man whispered to Father and then we saw Father turn away and hurry towards the part of the fortress where his senior officers stayed.

'Something is happening.' Dara said as we went up to the soldier, now leading his horse away towards the stable. As we got closer I recognized him. He was one of Father's most loyal men, a Rajput soldier who for a while was on duty guarding the Mahal gate in Agra. Here he is trusted enough to guard the women and escort Mother when she leaves the fort in her covered palanquin.

I ran up to him. 'Chait Singhji!' He turned a tired face towards us and smiled slightly, 'Ah! My little Flower Begum! What are you doing out so early?'

I smiled back at him, remembering how he used to call me Flower Begum because he said my face reminded him of an opening rose.

'What is happening, Chait Singhji?' Dara asked in his impatient way.

He grinned, his white teeth gleaming against the dusty brown skin, 'Well, the royal messenger has arrived, Prince Dara. They will be at the fort gate by mid morning. I had to ride very fast to get here before them.'

I stood still, my heart thudding. I turned away and went into Sati-un-nissa's room and sat down near her.

'Chait Singh says the royal messenger will be here this morning.'

She glanced at my face and said, 'Go and write your diary, it will keep you busy.' And then she bustled out to inform Mother.

That evening

The day has gone by in a storm of confusion and excitement and I am still feeling a bit shaken by it. I do not even know if I feel relieved or sad at the turn our lives have taken. I just know I am so afraid for my brothers Dara and Aurangzeb...

Father chose to receive the royal messenger in the palace sitting room, the baithak, that he had turned into his court hall. This formal sitting room was very well furnished and here he gave audience to the local people, sitting on his low cushioned seat. Listening to their petitions, passing orders, receiving and sending his letters to the Emperor.

I knew Mother and Sati-un-nissa planned to be there in the durbar hall when the royal messenger arrived. Whenever Mother decides to attend the durbar, one corner of the baithak is curtained off, so she can sit there, out of sight of the gathering men, and still be able to see and hear everything.

Dara and I were determined we were not going to be left behind, whatever happened. We kept loitering outside Mother's room, so we wouldn't miss her. When Mother came out it was an hour before noon. The royal messenger was due to arrive within the hour. She and Sati-un-nissa had veiled themselves and came out together wearing the all-covering robes. Dara and I said nothing. We just started walking beside them.

Mother turned her head to look at us and I could see her eyes behind the veil. 'What do you think you two are doing?'

'Can we come with you please, Mother, please?' I pleaded.

'I have to be there. It is important.' Dara said in a very superior voice.

'Oh is it? Why does an eleven-year-old have to attend the court? To talk to the royal messenger yourself?' Mother sounded both impatient and amused.

Dara realizing his mistake quickly apologized. 'Forgive me, Ammi, but Jahan and I really want to be there.'

Mother stood there as if unable to make up her mind. Then Sati-un-nissa spoke. 'Let them come, Princess. They are anxious, too.' Then she turned her dark veiled head towards us. 'You will sit quietly and watch from behind the curtain. Also, don't tell your father we took you there.'

As we began to walk through the palace corridors, towards the durbar hall, Mother asked Sati-un-nissa, 'Do you think the children should witness what may happen today?'

'Yes. Their lives are going to be affected too.'

'But they are so young!' Mother protested.

'Not really. Your husband was going off to war at fifteen; Akbar was a king and a general at thirteen. Mughal children grow up early.'

They walked on in silence for a while and then Mother sighed and said softly, 'Oh Sati, Khurram has lost his fight with the Emperor. Now if Nur Jahan is not merciful...'

I felt very scared hearing the worry in her voice. Mother who was always so calm and brave was afraid, and Sati-un-nissa had no words to console her.

We entered the durbar hall through a side door and went and sat in the curtained enclosure where carpets and cushions had been

laid out on the floor. It was screened off from the hall by a reed curtain. It was dim and dark in there, so looking through the reed curtain we had a clear view of the lighted hall outside.

The durbar hall was filling up with Father's men. I saw Father's adviser Abdur Rahim Khan-i-Khanan, an old, white-bearded man. He is one of the most important noblemen in Jahangir's court who had chosen to support Father against the Empress. Then there were officers, generals and men from the administrator's office. Dara pointed out some men who were local officials from Mandu.

Officially, Father was still the governor of the southern province of the Dakhan and Mandu was his provincial capital. So the Mandu officers must have come to see if he would remain their governor after the arrival of the Emperor's royal order.

His crime was that he had refused an order of the Emperor to take his army to the north to fight the Shah of Persia. The Shah had occupied the city of Kandahar, the northernmost part of the Mughal Empire.

An angry Jahangir had abandoned his expedition to save Kandahar and instead sent his second son Pervez with an army to attack Father. The two armies had met at Fatehpur Sikri near Agra and Father was defeated. Since then Prince Pervez and the Mughal general Mahabat Khan have been chasing Father across the kingdom.

They have met in battle many times. Sometimes Father won, at others he lost. Then after four years of wandering around the kingdom, being chased by the imperial forces, Father grew so weary that he finally sued for peace. The royal messenger carries the reply from the Emperor. Father was yet to arrive. His seat was empty. I knew he would wait in the side chamber until the guests were at the door and then make a grand entry. Appearances were very important for a royal audience.

There was a low hum of conversation around the room, like the buzzing of a hundred bees. Once in a while a man would glance towards the curtained corner where we sat and then quickly turn his head away. It would be very unseemly

to stare at us but they were obviously wondering if Mother was sitting there.

Silence reigned in our corner. I saw Mother's fingers move around her pearl prayer beads but I could not see her veiled face. What could happen to Father? I wondered.

There was movement at one of the side doors and Father came in. He walked up to take his seat on the throne as the men in the room bowed low before him. I noticed he was wearing his best jewels—the ornament of the sarpech, a triangle of jewels gleamed on his turban. His best strings of pearls lay across his chest and his fingers glowed with rings. He looked so handsome as he sat on the seat and waved to the soldiers at the door and said, 'Let the royal messenger come in!'

All our eyes turned to the main door. Dara leaned forward eagerly, parting the reeds of the curtain to get a better view. Even Mother's fingers had stilled around the prayer beads for a moment. We heard the call of the guards at the door announcing the guests.

The royal messenger walked into the hall

with a flourish of his long dark cloak, followed by half a dozen men. He was a tall, fair man in a high silk turban. He wore a scarlet brocade robe over his loose trousers, with the silk belt called a kamarbandh tied around his waist. A small, jeweled dagger was thrust through the belt. The loose sleeves of his robe flowed before him as he bowed before Father, touching his forehead in a salute.

'Greetings, Your Highness!'

The messenger stood before Father. One of his men handed him a long, round, silken case, which he opened and drew out a roll of parchment paper. He opened it and said, 'Greetings from Emperor Nuruddin Jahangir to his son Prince Khurram.'

Father bowed. 'My greetings to my father and my king, I sincerely hope he is keeping well.'

'He went to Kashmir to recover his health, sire. Now he is in Lahore and is feeling better.'

'I thank Allah for that.' Father leaned forward slightly, his voice was calm.

The royal messenger began to read,
Allah be praised.

The men in the hall echoed his prayer.

In the praise of Allah, I, Nuruddin Jahangir, Emperor of Hindustan send my greetings to my son Khurram-Shah Jahan.

It was a matter of great distress to me that my son chose to disobey my orders. The Empire needed his services as a general and he refused to provide them.

However, it pleases me to know that he has realized the mistake of his ways and has called upon my mercy.

It is my wish that my son Prince Khurram is hereby divested of his jagir of Hissar-Firoz, which I now present to my son Prince Shahriyar. Prince Khurram will now have the jagir of Balochpur instead of Hissar-Firoz. He is also to surrender the forts of Rohtas and Asir, which are now in his possession.

The royal messenger paused to take his breath and in the moment of silence, I could hear the hiss of whispered conversation around me. I looked in surprise at Dara. Hissar-Firoz was Father's personal fiefdom; the jagir was always presented to the prince favoured by the king, the heir apparent.

During the reign of his father Akbar,

my grandfather Jahangir had Hissar-Firoz. If Shahriyar had Hissar-Firoz now, it meant he was the favoured son and now the heir apparent. Father's face showed no emotions as he waited for the rest of the order to be read out to him.

The royal messenger began to read again.

As he has himself begged for my forgiveness, I once again appoint him as the governor of the province of Dakhan.

I heard Mother give a small sigh of relief and sit up straight. Outside, I saw Abdur Rahim smile and nod in agreement.

He is to stay in the Deccan till it pleases me to ask him to travel anywhere else.

Dara turned and gave me a quick flashing smile. Our fears had proved wrong. You don't blind a man if you appoint him the governor of a province. So Father was obviously not meeting the same fate as my uncle Khusru. Neither was he being taken prisoner by the Emperor's men and taken to Agra in chains. He was still free and he would live.

'Oh Allah, thank you for listening to my prayers,' I prayed. 'Thank you from my heart.'

However, the royal messenger had not finished. He raised his voice again.

It is my hope that my son will now show me the loyalty that he had once given me so freely. However...

The man paused to clear his throat and I felt my heartbeat speed up.

To ensure that such an act of rebellion is not contemplated again, I order Prince Khurram to send two of his sons to join me at my court in Lahore. They are to travel back with my messenger.

'Allah!' Mother's voice rose in a wail of distress.

The messenger was still reading.

He can rest assured that the safety of my grandsons will be of the highest interest to me and to Empress Nur Jahan. They will always remain at my side.

Dara turned to look at Mother. 'Ammi, what does this mean?' His eyes had widened in fear. 'Will I have to go?'

Meanwhile in the court, Father had come down from his seat. His face was pale but his lips were firm. He walked up to the royal messenger and took the royal order from him. He kissed the order and touched it to his forehead.

'The wishes of His Majesty are my command. I will obey all his orders.'

The royal messenger bent low, touching his forehead with his hand. 'Personally, Your Highness, I am deeply happy that the disagreement between you and the Emperor has finally been resolved.'

Father waved to two of his men, 'Please escort our guests to their rooms. It has been a long journey. I hope you will take some rest as my guest here. Mandu is a beautiful place.'

'I have been told to return as quickly as I can.'

'Of course. But even His Majesty would not deny you a few days of rest after the successful completion of your task.'

The man smiled and bowed. Then he said a little apologetically, 'And the young princes...'

'When you are ready to leave, rest assured,' Father's voice was surprisingly calm, 'my sons will travel with you.'

Then he wheeled around and left the room.

I sat there in a daze and then I felt Sati-un-nissa touch my shoulder and got up to leave. The court hall was emptying rapidly. Dara

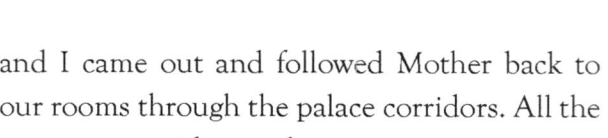

and I came out and followed Mother back to our rooms through the palace corridors. All the way no one said a word.

Entering her room Mother flung off her burqa and said, 'Sati, this is the work of the Empress. I know it!'

Sati-un-nissa nodded. 'I agree. Ordering Prince Khurram to send his sons as hostages has the clever touch of Nur Jahan. The Emperor would never think of taking away the boys like this. It is not his way.'

'True. But do not forget, he has agreed to the suggestions my aunt made and he has himself signed the royal order.'

Mother sat down and looked at Dara, standing by the door, and seemed to answer the question he had asked her at the durbar hall. 'Oh Dara, I don't know! We have to wait for your father to decide.'

Hearing our voices, Roshanara, Shuja and Aurangzeb came rushing in and were told about the royal order. I saw their faces fall when they heard about the order to send two of the boys to Agra.

Two days later

Father has decided that Dara and Aurangzeb will go with the royal messenger. They are supposed to be the invited guests of our grandfather Jahangir and will be living with him, but we all know that they are going as hostages—to make sure that Father behaves himself and never declares war against Grandfather again.

I hate him. I hate my grandfather for being so cruel, separating two boys from their mother. Did he even think about what my poor brothers would face, living alone in the Mughal harem? But I hate my grandaunt Nur Jahan even more. Because we all know it is she who has devised this terrible plan to keep my father obedient to the will of the Emperor.

Dara being the oldest son, had to go. I was expecting that. He is, after all, eleven years old and can take care of himself. But I don't understand why it has to be Aurangzeb. He is just eight, and I don't know why he has been chosen to go instead of Shuja.

Last Sunday after the farman had been read at the durbar, Father did not come to our rooms for lunch. He was in the durbar hall with his advisers till evening. Mother, who had been weeping a lot, was quite exhausted and went to bed. Sati-un-nissa stayed beside her.

Dara and I wandered about the garden, waiting for Father to come.

'I am the eldest. I am sure I will have to go.' Dara said gloomily, kicking a stone.

I was silent. I knew he was right.

'Murad is too young. You and Roshanara are girls. So it is among the three of us.' He sat down on the grass, crossed his arms, as if he was feeling cold in the sunny spring day. 'I know I'll be the first to be chosen by Father. Probably, it will be Shuja and me.'

'I think so, too.' I sat down next to him and put an arm around his shoulders. 'I'll ask Abbu. Maybe I can also go with you and Shuja.'

He turned, looking hopefully at me. 'Will you?'

I nodded. Then we saw Father come down the path and go towards Mother's rooms.

That night

Father spoke to Mother for a long time. At times I could hear their raised voices, Mother's in protest and Father trying to soothe her. I could hear her weeping again. Then Father came to the door and called us in. As the five of us entered, I saw Mother quickly wipe her eyes and sit up straight with a slightly shaky smile.

Father looked at our faces and said, 'You all know what is happening. All the other conditions laid down by my father I have found easy to accept. But I do not agree with his order that I send my sons to Agra.'

'But you cannot disobey him.' Aurangzeb, as always, was working out all the options, like a smart chess player. I have noticed before that he thinks quickly and seldom gets very excited or angry.

'I am ready to go, Abbu.' Dara said firmly.

'So am I,' said Shuja.

'And I,' said Aurangzeb.

I was so proud of my brothers. None of them were looking scared.

Father smiled. 'Shabash! That is the way to

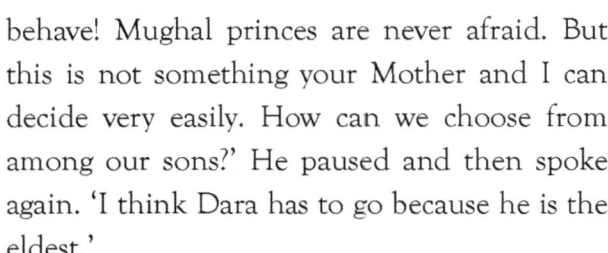

behave! Mughal princes are never afraid. But this is not something your Mother and I can decide very easily. How can we choose from among our sons?' He paused and then spoke again. 'I think Dara has to go because he is the eldest.'

Dara swallowed but nodded, trying to look brave.

'Who else? Me?' Shuja wanted to know.

To my surprise, Father turned to Aurangzeb and said, 'And will you be a brave young prince and go with Dara, Aurangzeb?'

Aurangzeb nodded mutely.

'But he is younger than me, Abbu!' Shuja protested.

'I know. But both your mother and I feel Aurangzeb, who is very smart, will be the right one to go. I need one of my older sons beside me here in the Deccan. So you, Shuja, will stay here to help me.'

As always, Father had put it so subtly that no one was hurt. But I still did not understand why Aurangzeb had to go.

'Abbu,' I began carefully, 'Aurangzeb is

only eight and he does not keep well.' Father nodded. 'Wouldn't it be better if I went with him? I could take care of him and Dara and the three of us could stay in the harem quite comfortably.'

'Yes, please!' Aurangzeb pleaded, looking a little relieved.

Father gave an impatient shake of his head. 'Don't be a fool, Jahan! I cannot allow you to travel alone with the royal messenger.'

'Why not?' I asked, feeling very puzzled.

'Because you are a girl.' It was Mother who replied instead of Father.

'No daughter of mine will travel alone without her parents.' Father decisively ended all discussions.

I glanced at Aurangzeb's disappointed face. His eyes were filled with tears. I saw him bend his head to hide them from us.

Next Friday morning
I woke up very early this morning and couldn't fall asleep again. Nowadays, I always fall asleep and wake up counting the days. I wonder how

much longer Father will be able to keep the royal messenger waiting.

The messenger has not protested yet, or started planning his journey. He is enjoying a well-deserved rest and Father's men are making sure the men in the royal entourage are kept well entertained. There have been musical soirees and dance performances. Often, they all go off riding or hunting. Still, one day they will have to start their journey back.

With my heart sinking, I keep counting the days as they pass. What will I do when Dara leaves? Who will I talk to? He is my only friend in Mandu.

I did not like the feeling of lying in bed, with all my worries crowding my head, like a bunch of evil demons. Why is it that the worries seem worse at night? I decided it was time to get up. It was already getting light outside.

Everyone was still asleep. Roshanara was curled up into a ball beside me. I peered into the boys' room. Dara was just a hump under the quilt; Shuja lay sprawled across his bed. Then I realized that Aurangzeb's bed was empty. I

looked around, feeling worried. Where had he gone? I wanted to ask Sati-un-nissa but she was at her prayers.

I decided to go in search of Aurangzeb. No one saw me when I walked out of the back door. Not even the guard who sat dozing by the wall, his spear lying slack against his arm. As I crept past him, I heard him snore and it made me smile. I searched in the garden where Aurangzeb usually played but he was nowhere.

I walked to the back of the Jahaz Mahal Palace, it had a large pool called Chandralok. Mandu has two lakes, set like silver plates between the palaces and they are really beautiful. The trees and the walls of the palaces are reflected in the still waters like a pretty painting. In the evenings, I often sit by these lakes with Sati-un-nissa and as the sun sets, we watch the waters turn a burnished gold and then dip quickly into an inky darkness.

I found Aurangzeb's tiny hunched figure sitting by the pool, as he stared moodily across the water. He had not heard my footsteps on the grass and looked up startled when I sat down

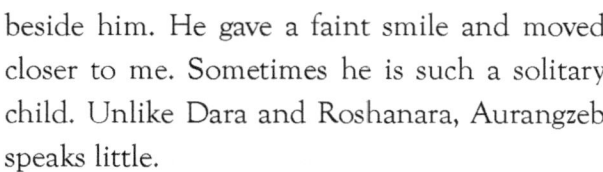

beside him. He gave a faint smile and moved closer to me. Sometimes he is such a solitary child. Unlike Dara and Roshanara, Aurangzeb speaks little.

'You are awake very early, Zeb.'

'Couldn't sleep.'

'I couldn't sleep either. I keep counting the days...'

He was silent for a while and then said in his soft way, 'Jahan Apa, why did Abbu choose to send me to Agra instead of Shuja?'

'Because, as he said, you are smarter than Shuja. And I agree with him.'

He shook his head, 'That was just an excuse. He did not want me to be here and have both Dara and Shuja gone.'

The sadness in his voice surprised me. 'What? Why do you think that, Zeb?'

He did not answer my question. Instead he asked, 'Apa, why does Abbu dislike me so much?'

'What made you think that?'

'It is true. He loves you and Dara the most. Whenever you speak to him, he smiles but he gets so angry when I ask him anything.'

'Well you do ask very strange questions, Zeb.' I tried to change the subject. 'Sometimes very embarrassing ones too that make Abbu angry.'

His face brightened and he began to smile.

'Remember the time when we were in Udaipur? The Rana of Mewar had come to visit and right in front of all the royal men of Mewar you wanted to know why Rajputs only grew their moustaches and never their beards.'

Aurangzeb began to grin. 'And Abbu said that at least they have moustaches. You, Zeb, have nothing!'

I stood up and pulled up Aurangzeb and we walked back to the palace. He walked absently, holding my hand. I thought, what he said is not completely wrong. Somehow, he always manages to rub Father the wrong way. But did Father choose to send him instead of Shuja because he did not like him? I found that hard to believe. But my little brother is hurt and confused and no one, neither my parents, nor Sati-un-nissa have taken the trouble to explain anything to him.

Aurangzeb looked up at me. 'Can I ask you something, Jahan Apa?'

I gave a mock groan. 'Here we go!'

He ignored my protests, his face screwed up in a thoughtful frown. 'Abbu is Grandfather's favourite son, isn't he?' I nodded. 'He is also the best general among the royal princes. Uncle Khusro is dead; Pervez and Shahriyar are pretty useless, aren't they? Uncle Pervez drinks all the time and Shahriyar is sort of stupid.'

'Don't say that before Ammi.' I knew what was coming next.

He smiled but continued. 'Abbu is by far the best of the royal princes. Then why does the Empress not want Abbu to become the next king when Grandfather dies? Why does she support Shahriyar?'

'This is a question, Prince Aurangzeb,' I began to drag him to our rooms, 'that I cannot answer on an empty stomach. Let's hurry for breakfast.'

'But then, you will have to tell me.'

'I know that, My Troublesome Prince.'

I gave a loud sigh that made him laugh.

That afternoon

My brothers have all gone riding, so I have managed to avoid Aurangzeb and his questions. But I have been thinking about it. What made Nur Jahan lose her faith in Father? Why did she suddenly choose to favour Prince Shahriyar instead? An odd choice!

I thought of Prince Shahriyar, the youngest of Jahangir's four sons. Because his mother was only an unimportant concubine and not a princess, he was not given the same honours as his brothers. I always found him a bit odd and Dara agrees with me. Dara is convinced Shahriyar is a bit weak in the head. He has this really strange laugh, like the neighing of a horse and he sniggers at the most embarrassing moments. I always thought both Grandfather Jahangir and Nur Jahan found him boring.

Today I carried my paper, pen and ink back to the balcony. I find I am happiest writing here. I like the breeze on my face and looking out across the garden to the silver shimmer of the lake. At one time Grandfather Jahangir was very fond of Mandu.

In those happy days, he and the Empress would gather the family and come to Mandu to see the rains. There would be open-air picnics by the lake and musicians playing all the time. Nowadays, he prefers to go to Kashmir. He loves the mountains and says that he feels better and breathes more easily in the clear air. I think if it had been possible, he would have preferred to have his capital in Kashmir and never return to hot and dusty Agra.

Evening

A few moments ago, Mother told us that we are going on a pilgrimage tomorrow. There is the shrine of a Sufi saint in the nearby town of Dhar and she wants to take all of us there before Dara and Aurangzeb leave for the north.

The trip to Dhar and back will take us about a week. I think Mother is stalling for time and she is trying to postpone the departure of the boys. When the royal messenger was told of her plans he may not have been pleased but he could hardly refuse a princess her wish to visit the dargah of a great Sufi pir. Father is not

coming with us. Instead, we are to be escorted by the trusted Chait Singh and his Rajput soldiers.

I like visiting the shrines of Sufi saints. They are such joyous places. There is the shrine of Sheikh Muinuddin Chishti in Ajmer and of Salim Chishti in Fatehpur Sikri. My favourite is the dargah of Sheikh Nizamuddin Auliya in Dilli.

There, every morning and evening, qawwali singers perform in the main courtyard and the people sing and clap with them. The place is always decorated with fragrant garlands and incense perfumes the air. Then, sometimes, when the music and the beat of the drums become faster, some of the devotees begin to sway and dance. Dara and I like the songs of the Sufis, full of the love of god and kindness and love for people.

As I wrote the last few lines, I had unconsciously begun to hum one of my favourite qawwallis, *Chhaap tilak sub chhini re mosay nainn milaikay*...It was a song written by the great poet Amir Khusro for his beloved Sufi

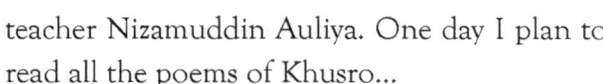

teacher Nizamuddin Auliya. One day I plan to read all the poems of Khusro...

The maid came out to tell me that dinner was served, and it is getting too dark to write anyway. Tomorrow, we travel to Dhar.

Tonight, I have to choose the clothes I want to take with me. I definitely want to wear my blue and silver gharara with the short top and the dupatta that is set with tiny silver stars to cover my head. Sati-un-nissa had made me stitch hundreds of these *salma sitaras* (special stars) on the gossamer thin cloth of the light blue veil. It had taken me weeks and weeks to do. But now the dupatta does look very pretty—like the inky-blue night sky dotted with sparkling stars.

I may not get the time to write while we travel to Dhar. I will come back and write again. During our pilgrimage I must look at everything very carefully and remember them all.

Oh! The maid has come to call me again... I better go...she told me there is my favourite korma and pulao for dinner...

On the way to Dhar

We began our journey early in the morning.
The women and girls travelled in two covered
horse carriages. The boys rode on horses or if
they felt tired they could join us in the carriages.
Aurangzeb, not feeling too well, decided to
travel with Roshanara and me.

We were escorted by soldiers led by Chait
Singh. Dhar was a day's journey from Mandu
and we were to set up camp there for a few days.
Mother was carrying a chaader, a silk covering
embroidered in gold, that she planned to lay
over the grave of the saint, Pir Kamal Maula.

The day was just beginning as we set out.
The sun was a whisper of pink and orange on
the eastern horizon and the birds were still
fluttering and calling around the trees. I peered
out of the curtains of the carriage. We were
moving down the road from the fort, on top
of a hill. All around were endless stretches of
green forests and some patches of fields around
a huddle of village huts.

The royal entourage usually moves slowly.
It is such an unwieldy thing. There are soldiers

on horseback, carriages for the women, bullock carts carrying our luggage, tents, kitchen things and sacks of grain, spices and vegetables. The maids, servants, and cooks travel on the carts. And everything moves at a slow, meandering pace.

When the royal army moves, there are also elephants, camels, cannons, and marching soldiers. The villagers line the sides of the road to watch the army pass and sometimes the procession goes on for days. Whenever Father is in a hurry, he sends off men who set up the tents a couple of days ahead, so that the camp is ready when he arrives. Meanwhile, another team of camp officials moves on to the next halt to begin work. Sometimes, the army on the move has more servants, officials, and their families than soldiers who will actually do the fighting. An army camp becomes like a small town with bazaars selling all kinds of wares.

The narrow track wound its way through a forest and when it neared a village, the children came running up to stare at us. I watched a man ploughing his field, one thin bullock pulling

the wooden plough. Our villagers are so poor, the children are thin and nearly naked. Mother and Sati-un-nissa had a bag of copper coins and they were throwing them among the children who scrambled in the dust to pick them up.

We travelled all day, stopping only for meals. It was dark by the time we reached Dhar. We were to stay in a serai, a small inn near the shrine, and the tents were set up outside for the soldiers and the kitchens. We children were so tired, we all fell asleep and had to be woken up to eat a very late dinner.

In Dhar

Next morning we walked to the shrine, the dargah of the Sufi saint Pir Kamal Maula. It was a small shrine. The grave was in a simple marble pavilion surrounded by an open courtyard. Mother and Sati-un-nissa laid the silk chaader over the grave and covered it with rose petals. We all said our prayers. I begged Pir Sahib to take care of Dara and Aurangzeb.

Right next to the dargah was a small room where a holy man stayed and it was said that

he could see the future. I saw Mother and Sati-un-nissa enter his room and I followed them. I sat down just outside the door where they could not see me but I could hear what the man said.

I knew my parents often consulted astrologers to find the right time to do any important thing. Maybe, Mother wanted to find out the day when the boys should leave for Agra. So I was quite surprised to hear her first question—

'Huzoor,' she began, speaking from behind her veil, 'I need to know the future of my four sons.'

Sati-un-nissa silently handed over four rolls of parchment, which must have been the birth charts of my brothers. I peered in and saw a man in a turban and with a long white beard hold the charts against the light from a window and study them carefully for a very long time and then he spoke—

'Begum Sahiba, I know you are worried about sending your sons away. We in Dhar have come to know of the Emperor's farman.'

'My children are entering the harem ruled by my aunt Nur Jahan. I do believe she would not harm them herself, but my husband's enemies at court would not hesitate. My heart is filled with fear.'

The old man spoke in a quiet, kind way, smiling slightly behind his beard, 'You can rest assured, the boys will be safe, and as I see in their charts, they will be restored to you...'

'Oh thank you! Praise be Allah!' Mother's voice was breathless with relief.

The old man smiled. 'The boys have many more years to live.'

Then he raised his head and seemed to look straight at Mother's veiled face. I noticed his large, deep-set eyes, set under bushy white brows, and their fierce, penetrating gaze.

'Your third son, Aurangzeb...' the old man spoke again.

'Huzoor, he has a weak constitution and often does not keep well.'

The man shook his head. 'He has a long lifeline, you need not worry. I just feel that you and the prince...' he paused, as if choosing the right words, and then spoke very carefully, '...be very kind, patient and loving to this boy...teach him to love his brothers.'

There was a moment's silence as if Mother was trying to understand what the man was saying. 'What are you telling me?' she finally asked.

The old man bent his head. 'I see conflict and anger in his life. These two charts of brothers do not harmonise. Of him and his brother Dara.'

Sati-un-nissa spoke for the first time. 'Huzoor, it is the fate of the Mughal men that brother fights brother for the throne. Even sons rise against their father. It is quite possible that in the future these brothers may go to war.'

The man nodded, still staring down at the chart. 'There is so much anger and bitterness in this child, I do not understand it.' He turned to Mother. 'Is he not loved, Begum Sahiba?'

'He is loved. They are all loved.' Mother's voice was filled with sadness. 'Huzoor, I am a Mughal princess and this is the burden I carry with me. That one day my sons will rise against each other...it is inevitable.' She paused. 'When

Aurangzeb was born and the court astrologer was drawing his charts, he warned my husband that the child could one day prove to be a danger to him,' her voice sank, 'and you are saying the same. Still, he is my son and I love him.'

The old man said softly, 'These charts only show possibilities, Begum Sahiba, What they say is what could happen in the future but our futures are not written in stone. Once we know what can happen, we can work to avoid the pitfalls.'

Mother bowed and said her thanks, as Sati-un-nissa laid a small bag of coins before the old man. I got up and slipped away quickly before they came out. I did not want them to see me.

On the walk back home, I thought I finally knew the answer to Aurangzeb's question. He had asked me why Father disliked him. Father believes deeply in the astrologers, and their predictions about Aurangzeb being unlucky for him, he would not forget easily.

Now I know why Father chose to send Aurangzeb and not Shuja to the Emperor. But

how could Father forget that what was written in Aurangzeb's chart was not his fault? My brother was just eight years old, how could Father be angry with him? Sometimes, I do not understand adults at all.

I am just a daughter, I cannot ask him anything. I wonder if Mother has ever questioned Father. I cannot bear the thought of my brothers fighting each other for the throne. Still, the old man's words had calmed some of my fears. He sounded so sure that Dara and Aurangzeb would be safe. Even Mother had become calmer and I heard her tell Sati-un-nissa that now she would be able to sleep at night.

We stayed in Dhar for three days. Mother and Sati-un-nissa would go to the shrine everyday to pray and they often took the boys with them. One night we heard the qawwali singers perform, singing in praise of god, and as they sang a man from the audience got up to dance. It was all very pleasing but sitting there beside my brothers, my heart was heavy.

I am learning something at Dhar. It is not easy being a Mughal princess. For all the luxuries of my Mother's life, she lives in fear for the life of her husband and her sons. Just as I fear for my father and brothers. And the hardest thing is that they may not always listen to our advice.

Back in Mandu

We reached Mandu last evening. Father was waiting for us at the palace door and helped Mother climb down from the carriage—long rides tire her badly. We were all quite stiff from the ride. I was so tired, I fell asleep the moment my head touched the pillow.

This morning, Dara and I decided to visit some of our favourite haunts within the Mandu fortress one final time before he left. We knew the time of his leaving was drawing near. I had seen the carriages and carts being prepared for the long journey to Agra.

Both Dara and I love the palace called Hindola Mahal. It is built with walls that slope inwards at a sharp angle that makes it seem as if the stone palace is swaying in the breeze, like a swing tied to a tree.

'One day,' Dara said, 'I want to build a palace

like this in Agra. With a lake beside it, filled with lotus flowers.'

I laughed. 'A lake in dry and hot Agra?'

'I know. That is the problem. Even that lake that Badshah Akbar built at Fatehpur Sikri dried up.'

We wandered through the rooms of the Hindola Mahal. 'You could do something else,' I smiled at his dreamy face. 'You could shift your capital to Mandu when you become king.'

'If I am king...' Dara said moodily as we walked through the palace rooms. 'Who knows if I ever will be king.'

'You are the eldest son.'

'So was Uncle Khusro. Look what happened to him.'

'Do you know Father is planning a banquet?' I quickly changed the subject, trying to cheer him up. 'They are getting the best singers of Mandu to come and sing.'

Dara pointed to the palace called Rupmati Mahal and said, 'They say Rupmati would sing to Baz Bahadur there in that palace.'

Dara and I are fascinated by the story of the

tragic romance of Nawab Baz Bahadur and his queen Rupmati. During the early years of the reign of my great-grandfather Akbar, Mandu was the capital of the independent kingdom of Malwa, and Baz Bahadur was the nawab. The problem with Baz Bahadur was that he was a better singer than a ruler. He liked to spend his time singing, listening to musicians, and composing songs. He himself had a very beautiful voice and so he and his beloved queen, the beautiful Rupmati, spent their days with music.

Akbar, who was keen to expand his kingdom sent his general Adham Khan to conquer Malwa. Fearing a battle he couldn't win, Baz Bahadur ran away, leaving Rupmati behind at Mandu. Adham Khan captured Mandu, and the women in Baz Bahadur's harem became his prisoners.

Adham Khan was cruel. He ill-treated Baz Bahadur's noblemen and the harem women. Many of Mandu's noblemen were killed and the women were made slaves. One night, Adham Khan summoned Rupmati to his room. When

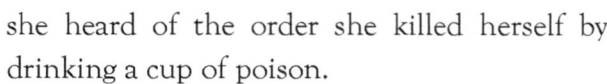

she heard of the order she killed herself by drinking a cup of poison.

Reports of Adham Khan's misbehaviour reached Agra, and Akbar was furious. It is a tradition among the Mughals that during war they never harm women or children. The women of the harem were always treated with the greatest respect. So Akbar decided to go to Mandu himself.

Adham Khan was Akbar's foster brother as his mother Maham Anaga had been Akbar's nurse. Realizing that her son was in trouble, she sent a messenger to warn him of the arrival of Akbar. However, Akbar rode so fast he arrived even before Maham Anaga's messenger. He took away all the treasures that Adham Khan had won in the war and ordered him back to Agra in disgrace. Adham Khan could have faced the death penalty for killing the people of Mandu. He was only spared because his mother begged Akbar for mercy.

However, stubborn Adham Khan did not learn his lesson from the events at Mandu. A few years later, he killed Akbar's prime minister,

Atkah Khan. This time, Akbar was not going to listen to any prayers for mercy. He ordered that Adham Khan be thrown off the walls of the Agra Fort. He did not die the first time so he was thrown off again to make sure he died.

The Mughal kings are benevolent despots. They are often merciful but their anger and vengeance can be terrible. I have seen the same trait of ruthlessness in Akbar's son and my grandfather, Emperor Jahangir. His rage can be unbelievably cruel. Men have been trampled under elephants' feet and dragged behind horses till they died.

To come back to the tale of poor Baz Bahadur, he wandered around the country for a few years—a king without a kingdom, living off the kindness of other kings. Finally, he begged Akbar for peace and was welcomed into the Mughal court. He lived there for the rest of his life with all the honours and salary of a nobleman.

At his magnificent court at Fatehpur Sikri, Akbar had the two greatest singers of the land— Baz Bahadur and the legendary Mian Tansen.

I turned to Dara, 'Well, the singers at tonight's banquet may not be Baz Bahadur but still the music should be good.'

'A farewell to Mandu in song...' Dara made a tragic face and intoned in a loud dramatic voice, 'Goodbye, dear Mandu, goodbye rose garden and Hindola Mahal, alvida lotus pool and picnic by the lake...'

I laughed. He can be such a clown and I am going to miss him so much.

An entertainment

Father's banquet for the royal messenger was also a farewell party for Dara and Aurangzeb. Roshanara was excited for days. On the day of the banquet, she was troubling the maids from the morning about what she would wear—the clothes, jewellery, shoes and even the attar (perfume).

Roshanara had opened her box of clothes and laid out her best dresses on the carpet.

'Tell me Jahan, I can't decide between the red and the yellow.'

This was the third time she had asked me to choose from her dresses and I was tired of her game.

'Take any,' I said wearily. 'You'll look as silly in all of them.'

'What's wrong with you? Why are you in such a grumpy mood?' She gave me a glare. 'Father is throwing a banquet after months and all morning you have been sitting there doing that boring stitching.'

I looked up, the embroidery was giving me a headache. 'Don't you realize our brothers are leaving tomorrow?'

'I know. They'll have a good time in Agra, don't worry. The Empress will make sure of that.'

'The Empress wants them as hostages.'

'I know.' Roshanara's eyes gleamed. 'Isn't she clever?'

I don't understand my sister. I really don't.

That evening the great court by the Jahaz Mahal Palace was covered by a huge tent. The ground was covered by cotton spreads and over the dhurries were laid the soft silk Persian

carpets. As always, one part of the tent had been screened off for women.

Mother, Sati-un-nissa, Roshanara and I played hostess to the wives and daughters of Father's army commanders and of the Mandu officials. I walked beside the maids carrying the trays of sherbets and wines making sure everyone had something to drink.

The air was perfumed by incense and the fragrance of flowers. There were bunches of roses in the vases and marigold garlands snaked around the tent poles and swayed over the doorways. Outside, the shehnai players welcomed the guests with their music. Servants moved among the guests offering sherbet and wine, kababs and other savouries. Tall torches burned in the corners, lighting the tent with their golden light and making the shadows dance.

I watched the glittering scene from behind the reed curtains. Tonight, my brothers were allowed to join the men and I saw Abdur Rahim Khan-i-Khanan talking to Dara. Once he had been the tutor of my grandfather Jahangir

but now he had joined Father because of his disagreements with the Empress. Sati-un-nissa said he was a very special man—a great warrior, a respected courtier who had led many diplomatic missions for the Emperor and also a wonderful poet and scholar. I have read the poems that he writes under the pseudonym of 'Rahim'. Dara and I love to talk to the old man. He tells such fascinating stories.

Father sat among his courtiers with the royal messenger beside him. Then the singers and dancers came in to entertain the guests. First the principal singer, who was a disciple of Baz Bahadur, sang some numbers composed by his guru. Then two courtesans in their long, silk-pleated skirts and sparkling veils came out to dance to the music.

By the time the dances ended I noticed that the royal messenger had drunk many cups of wine. His face was flushed red and he was swaying and nodding drunkenly to the music. Father does not drink much, unlike Grandfather Jahangir and Uncle Pervez. He may take a glass of wine at banquets at the

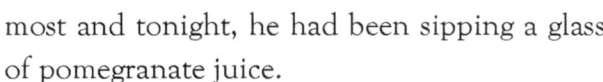

most and tonight, he had been sipping a glass of pomegranate juice.

Grandfather Jahangir of course also takes opium, so that I have seen him fall asleep in the middle of a banquet. Then the servants come up quietly and carry him away as the guests leave quickly. Maybe, Father does not drink because he has seen the effect of wine and opium on his father.

I watched the dancers twirl round and round with the wide skirts of their lehengas and the dupattas flaring out like the opening petals of a flower. Their heavy ankle bells jangled as they moved their feet to the beat of the drums. They had darkened their eyes with kohl and painted their lips and they glittered with jewellery and tinsel.

It was quite late by the time the men got up to eat and I noticed that many of them were swaying because of all the wine they had drunk. Trays of food were served to the ladies in a covered tent. At least six kinds of kababs, fragrant and spicy rice pulaos and biryanis, korma and kaliya of lamb and fish. The plates of

breads had paranthas, naans and bakarkhwani rotis. The dessert platter had phirni, kheer, many kinds of halwas, sweetmeats like barfis and laddus and the sweet rice zarda.

Dara, Shuja and Aurangzeb had come away to eat with us. So the five of us competed to see who could eat the most laddus and Shuja won by eating six of them. Roshanara ate so much she had to loosen the strings of her pyjamas and that made Sati-un-nissa laugh and recite a wicked poem.

A week later

Dara and Aurangzeb left four days ago. I wonder where they are now on the road to Agra. I did not feel like writing anything after they left and spent my time with Sati-un-nissa. She was busy supervising the maids who were putting away the winter clothes and taking out our summer dresses.

The thick quilted jackets and pashmina shawls, the quilts and woollen blankets were all packed away with camphor to protect them from moths. Now the lovely thin cottons came

out. Among them were two sets of kurtas and churidars that Nur Jahan had presented to me. They were embroidered with a delicate shadow work called chikankari.

My great aunt had created this special way of embroidery where the stitches are put on the reverse of the thinnest cotton and it shows through like a delicate shadow. She is really an amazing woman. She cooks, does embroidery, sings, writes poetry, paints and even goes hunting with my grandfather. She once shot a tiger from the howdah of an elephant.

The palace feels very empty without Dara and my time does not pass. It is not much fun to wander about alone in the gardens without anyone to talk to. How much painting, embroidery or reading can you do in a day after all?

Today, Father told us that we are to go to Nasik. He wants to set up his court there. So the packing has started again.

The Governor's Mansion
Nasik in the Deccan
Summer of 1626

In Nasik

WE ARE IN THE DECCANI TOWN of Nasik that stands by the banks of the Narmada. This place is not as beautiful as Mandu and now it is getting quite hot too. I wish I knew why Father shifted us all here.

I heard Mother and Sati-un-nissa discuss this.

Mother said, 'I do not understand Khurram at all nowadays. He is in such a strange humour. After the truce with his father we are in no danger, then why do we have to move again? And Nasik is even further from Agra.'

In the governor's haveli

We are staying in the best house in Nasik but it is nothing in comparison to the palaces of Mandu. It is a large mansion with two courtyards in the middle with two floors of rooms around them. Father has his durbar room and offices in the front courtyard, that is the mardana, or men's quarters, and we stay in the second, the zenana, or women's quarters.

There is very little to do here. I only have the back gardens to wander in and have to wait for the few trips out of the haveli. One day we went for a picnic by the banks of the Narmada on a boat. But now the summer sun makes it difficult to plan outings and Father has not been keeping well. There are days when he stays in the zenana to rest.

I moaned so much about getting bored that Mother asked Father to get me a tutor to give me lessons in Persian. The lady who comes to teach me is called Mahjabeen Khanum and she is very strict about her lessons. She teaches me Persian, grammar and mathematics. She also knows Sanskrit and I am thinking of learning

that too. I can read the Devanagri script so it should not be difficult to read, just that the words will have to be explained to me.

Mahjabeen Khanum came this morning carrying a bundle of illustrated manuscripts of poems. With her were two of her students who were girls my age. They are called Bilquis and Sundari and our tutor says we are to study together. I think Sati-un-nissa has worked this out. She knows how I long for friends. I am busy again and I also have two new friends. Roshanara and Shuja also join us for lessons, so the mornings pass quite quickly but in the evenings I miss my walks in Mandu with Dara.

Yesterday, after lessons, Bilquis and Sundari stayed back to play with Roshanara and me. They taught us a new game with six small stones called gittas. They were quite surprised that Roshanara and I did not know how to play it. It seems all the girls in the country play it. It is fun. You throw one stone in the air and quickly pick up the others before it comes down. Roshanara kept throwing the stone higher and higher and then couldn't catch it.

Bilquis and Sundari are daughters of officials in Nasik and are childhood friends. I think they are so lucky, I have never stayed anywhere long enough to make any friends and the last four years all we have done is travel. I have been to so many places—Lahore, Kashmir, Udaipur, Rohtas, Mandu, Burhanpur, Ajmer... My new friends think I am the lucky one because I have travelled to so many parts of the country. But even travelling can get very tiring.

One morning, as Mahjabeen Khanum was helping Sati-un-nissa with some letters, we were left alone and could forget the lessons and talk instead.

'Agra must be such a magnificent city,' Sundari said, 'Nasik is such a small and dull place.'

'You have travelled so much, which is your favourite place?' Bilquis asked.

'I think Udaipur was the best,' I said. 'It is the capital of the Rajput kingdom of Mewar and it is the most beautiful city I have ever seen.'

'We lived in a marble palace called Jag Mandir,' Roshanara added. 'It is built on an island in the middle of a lake.'

'What a lovely place to go for holiday!' Sundari said dreamily. 'Our holidays usually mean we go on pilgrimages.'

I laughed. 'It was not really a holiday. We were running away from the imperial army and Raja Karan Singh of Mewar gave us sanctuary.'

Roshanara grinned at the surprise on their faces. 'My uncle Pervez and the general Mahabat Khan were chasing us.'

'At the orders of my grandfather and my grand aunt,' I added.

'Your uncle was chasing you?'

'But your father is a prince!'

Roshanara and I were laughing so much we couldn't speak. We Mughals must seem to be very strange to other people.

Then Sundari said, 'But you all belong to the same family, don't you?'

That evening...

I felt like writing this evening because of what Sundari said. I couldn't forget the surprise in her eyes. Yes, Jahangir and Nur Jahan, Pervez and Shahriyar, we all belong to the same family.

Even the dead and forgotten Khusro was my uncle, my father's half-brother, my grandfather's eldest son. Once the heir apparent. If I had told them the tale, Bilquis and Sundari would have found it so hard to believe.

I cannot forget Khusro. Maybe because I do not know the whole story. No one, not my mother, my father or even Sati-un-nissa talk about him. I have heard the maids whisper his name but they go silent if they realize I can hear them. Dara and I have been told by Mother not to ask any questions and Father's face turns to stone if Khusro's name is mentioned in his presence.

Khusro was my grandfather's eldest son. He was the only child of Man Bai, who was Jahangir's first wife and a Rajput princess of Amber. He was born when Akbar was king and my grandfather was the crown prince. Among all his grandchildren, Akbar was most fond of Khusro and my father. In the forty-ninth year of his rule, when Akbar took ill, he was not expected to survive. At that time, Khusro was nineteen and my father was fifteen and there were many in the court who felt that Khusro and not Jahangir should be the next king.

In those final days of the rule of Akbar, there was much bitterness between him and his son Jahangir. My grandfather had rebelled many times, marching across the empire in defiance. There had been many reconciliations but Akbar was very unhappy and disappointed with his son. In contrast, Khusro was a handsome, popular young prince loved by Akbar. In a Mughal court, this meant a time of intrigue and trouble.

There were many in the royal court like Khusro's uncle, Man Singh, the Raja of Amber, who felt that he would make a better king than Jahangir. After all, my grandfather had not been a very successful heir apparent. He was not very energetic and disliked having to go on military expeditions. He preferred to spend his time in lazy pastimes with his friends and in the company of painters. He drank excessively and took opium. He had been feuding with Akbar for years and once had even declared himself the king in Allahabad. His stepmother Ruqaiyya Begum had to go there and drag him

back to Agra and force him to beg his father's forgiveness.

So there were two cliques at court—one supporting Jahangir and the other supporting Khusro, all gathered around the dying Akbar. Khusro was very young and he really began to believe that he would be the next king. So he was both angry and disappointed when Akbar on his deathbed anointed Jahangir as the next king. Khusro refused to accept this and declared war on his father.

The battle between father and son went on for quite a while but Khusro's was a lost cause. Grandfather had the imperial army behind him while poor Khusro only had his small band of loyal followers. His defeat was inevitable. When he was brought before Jahangir as a prisoner of war, Grandfather forgave him but Khusro refused to give up and rose in rebellion again.

Finally, Grandfather lost his temper and when Khusro was defeated and captured, he had his son blinded and imprisoned. Khusro was in prison for many years but he did manage to regain some of his sight. Then the women of

the family convinced Grandfather that Khusro had repented and begged him to let his son return to court. Among those who asked him was Nur Jahan and it was because she had her own plans for Khusro.

There were weeks of celebrations as Uncle Khusro was welcomed back to the court. He was a very charming man and very popular with our subjects, who all believed he would make a good king. I remember him as this handsome, smiling man who loved riding and hunting. His sight was still damaged but it did not stop him from doing anything. Many of the harem women were in love with him but he remained faithful to his only wife, the Princess Begum.

Nur Jahan's plan was simple. She wanted to marry her daughter Ladili Begum to Khusro. As Khusro was the eldest son, once he returned to Agra he would also become the heir apparent and would one day become king. So if he became her son-in-law, she could still rule the kingdom through him once Jahangir died. Khusro's mother Man Bai was already dead, which made things easier for Nur Jahan.

The Empress' plan went completely awry when Khusro stubbornly refused to marry Ladili Begum. Of course, Nur Jahan was not a person to give up easily and she married Ladili to Jahangir's youngest son, my uncle Shahriyar. Now Nur Jahan schemed and planned to make Shahriyar the heir apparent and poor Khusro became an obstacle in her path.

Five years ago, when Father was being sent on a military expedition to the south, he insisted that Khusro should accompany him. Nur Jahan supported him and so Khusro was made the head of the imperial forces with Father as his deputy. As this was a military expedition we children and Mother stayed behind in Agra. One day a letter arrived from Father, addressed to Jahangir, saying that Khusro had died of a stomach ailment.

Grandfather was extremely upset at the news. He was hopeful that Khusro had changed his ways and could one day follow him to the throne. I still remember the day the messenger arrived with the news of Khusro's death and how the palaces and the Mahal became silent in grief.

Grandfather withdrew into his bedchamber and refused to see anyone, not even Nur Jahan. He did not come out for two days. The Princess Begum who was Khusro's wife was surrounded by wailing women in the Mahal and the Rajput princesses all gathered in their prayer room to fast and pray for the soul of Khusro.

Then the rumours began. The Mahal is always full of gossip and intrigue and now the whispers were all aimed at Father. They began to say that Father had insisted on Khusro leading the forces to the south because he planned to kill his brother. They whispered that Khusro had been poisoned at Father's orders. Some of the men from Khusro's camp in the Deccan returned to Agra and they said that he had been given a slow poison in his food and drink and he had died slowly and very painfully.

It felt as if we were surrounded by a wall of anger and accusation. The women of the Mahal began to avoid us. Mother sat for days staring stonily out of the window and refused to speak to anyone. She sent Sati-un-nissa to Grandfather Jahangir, begging to be allowed to see him but

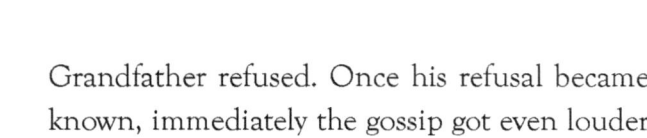

Grandfather refused. Once his refusal became known, immediately the gossip got even louder and more malicious.

One day I was in the garden, playing with Dara, and we heard two of the harem women talking on the other side of the garden hedge.

'I am not surprised at all,' one woman began, 'Khurram has never hidden the fact that he wants to be king.'

'When he took Khusro with him, he must have been planning something like this,' the other woman said.

'Now with Khusro gone, it is the poor, trusting Pervez who will be in danger,' the woman laughed, 'from his beloved half-brother.'

'How could he do this to a half blind man?'

'If the father can blind and imprison his son, why not?'

'Khusro made a mistake refusing Ladili's hand. It cost him his life.'

I heard the two begin to walk away, 'I wonder what Arjamand is thinking. The whole world believes Khurram is responsible. Brother against brother...these Mughal men...'

The voices were fading away but I still heard the last words, 'Poor Arjamand, don't forget, she has sons too.'

Dara and I had been sitting absolutely still. Now he turned his head and his eyes were wide with horror.

'What were they saying, Jahan? What did they mean about Father and Uncle Khusro?'

I could never hide anything from him. 'They are all saying Father had Uncle Khusro killed.'

'That is why Mother is in such a bad mood?'

I nodded.

We sat silent for a long while and then he asked, 'Do you believe what they are saying?'

'I don't know.'

And I still don't. No one has ever answered the question for us.

That night I went to Sati-un-nissa's room. She was sitting at her desk just staring absentmindedly into space.

'Sati Khanum,' I began, going to sit beside her on her cushion. 'Can I ask you something?'

She nodded and I had a feeling she knew what I was going to ask. Sometimes I think she can read my mind.

'I have been hearing the Mahal women talk...'

'I know what they are saying.' She reached out and pulled me closer. 'Jahan, I am only your Mother s companion, people don't tell me anything. I don't know what happened in the Deccan. How can I, sitting here in Agra?'

'But they are saying...'

'They will always say things. They are idle women with nothing to do except gossip and they are jealous of your mother who has a loving husband and a family.' She gave me a quick hug. 'You are a Mughal and they will always talk about you. So you have to ignore the gossip and think for yourself and not listen to what people say.' She looked out of the window and said musingly, 'These Mughal men do not know how to be kind but then, it is not easy to be a prince. When a Mughal king dies, there is no law that the eldest son becomes the king. So all his sons have to fight for the throne and either you become king or you are dead.'

'Did Grandfather do this too?'

She turned to look at me. 'Do you know how Abul Fazl was killed?'

'Abul Fazl? You mean Badshah Akbar's court historian?'

'Yes. He and Jahangir did not like each other. During the last days of Akbar's life there were two groups in court—one supporting Jahangir and the other Khusro. Abul Fazl supported the claims of Khusro to the throne. One day when Fazl was returning to Agra from the Deccan, Jahangir got his friend, the Raja of Orchha, to ambush and kill him.'

'Badshah Akbar knew about this?'

'Yes, and it broke his heart because Abul Fazl was among his closest friends. Akbar was so angry he nearly disinherited Jahangir and it was only at the request of the queens that he changed his mind.'

'So to become king, Grandfather first killed his father's best friend and then blinded and imprisoned his own son.'

'That is the way of the Mughals. The prince who is the strongest and the cleverest wins the throne.'

'And the other princes die?'

'It can happen.'

Then I think Sati-un-nissa thought she had said too much because she bundled me off to bed and refused to say anything more.

The next day I told Dara of my conversation with Sati-un-nissa. We both gathered what she was saying in her oblique way. That, it was possible that Father had Khusro poisoned. And that, it was nothing really surprising, the Mughal princes will always fight for the throne of Hindustan. Fight to their death.

I cannot forget Mother's still face framed by the window as she sat silent for days and ate very little. I knew she was afraid of the anger of the Emperor. She kept on sending requests for an audience with him and finally one day, the summons came.

Mother accompanied by Sati-un-nissa went to see Grandfather in Nur Jahan's palace. She had spent the night before praying. Dara and I were waiting for them at the door and it was such a relief to see her walk back smiling. The Emperor and Nur Jahan had been kind to her and not blamed Father for anything.

Still, I'll never forget that careless voice across

the garden hedge. 'Poor Arjamand! And don't forget she has sons too!'

Dara and I call Khusro 'Our uncle, the ghost'—the tragic soul that haunts our family. You would think one could not be more fortunate than being born a Mughal prince—all the power, wealth and luxury. Khusro's life is the real picture, and it is not a pretty one.

Khusro never got any love from his own father and mother. Man Bai was mentally imbalanced and killed herself when he was still quite young. Then he was imprisoned for years for his youthful folly and nearly became blind. And now he was dead, possibly at the hands of his own half-brother.

Rains in Nasik

The monsoon comes early in the south. In Agra it must be hot and dry still but here the world has turned a wet, emerald green. The garden has a fresh layer of sprouting grass that is soft as a silk carpet under my feet, the banana plant outside my window is shooting out new leaves and the droplets of rain are

caught on the lotus leaves in the pond, like translucent pearls.

I love the rains. In Agra, you wait and wait all through the endless summer months for the first grey clouds in the sky. On the day when the first showers arrive, there is celebration in the palaces. The Mahal women run out to get wet in the rain, they tie swings to the trees and special sweets are made.

In the rains there was a festival of the Hindus that the Rajput queens celebrated that I still remember. It was the birthday of their god, Lord Krishna and the biggest celebration was in the palace of my great-grandmother Mariam-us-Zamani. She was Akbar's first Hindu wife and the mother of his eldest son, Jahangir. So as the Queen Mother she was the most important person in the harem.

She was very old, a snowy-haired lady, always dressed in white. She would sit resting on cushions and we would go up to touch her feet and then she gave us small gifts. The Mahal was full of her grandchildren and great-grandchildren and she never forgot any of their

birthdays. I would get jewellery, and later when she discovered I like books, she would send me collections of poems and fairy tales.

On the birthday festival of Lord Krishna, her palace would be decorated with lamps and flowers, the floor painted in colourful patterns. In her prayer room was a silver throne made like a swing hanging by chains on which was an idol of the child Krishna made of gold and covered with jewellery. The Rajput princesses sang and danced before the idol and then Mariam-us-Zamani carried a lamp with many flames up to the silver throne and waved it before the idol as the priest chanted Sanskrit prayers. It was very beautiful and I enjoyed it as much as the Id and Navroz festivals.

A few days later

This morning it was raining so heavily that my tutor Mahjabeen Khanum could not come. So Roshanara, Shuja and I were playing in one of the outer rooms when we heard the horses. We looked up to listen because these horses were moving very fast and coming towards our haveli.

'Messengers?' Shuja asked as we tumbled out of the room.

'In this rain?' I wondered. 'It must be very important.'

When we reached the main door, two riders splashed with mud were getting off tired horses that were panting heavily. One of Father's officers had hurried out and the three of them stood and whispered for a moment. Then the officer said, 'Come inside now! His Highness is in his durbar room.' And the three ran quickly inside.

Roshanara turned to me, 'Something important has happened!'

'How do we find out?' Shuja wanted to know.

'I heard one man say Lahore...' I said.

'Lahore? An urgent message from the Emperor?'

We went and stood near the court room. After a while most of Father's most trusted men came hurrying in, many of them springing down from their horses, brushing the rain off their shoulders. The gathering went on all morning.

Father's steward and some waiters were

going in and out carrying trays of food and drinks. It was no use asking the steward because he wouldn't tell us. Then one of the younger waiters came out and we cornered him in the corridor.

'What's happening?' I asked anxiously.

'Message from Lahore?' Shuja asked.

'Is the Emperor dead?' Roshanara squeaked.

The man stopped at Roshanara's words and said, 'Of course not! I don't know exactly what has happened but Mahabat Khan has captured the Emperor and the Empress and is holding them prisoner in Lahore.'

The news was so surprising we were struck dumb, staring at each other. Then we were racing to the zenana to tell Mother the news. I immediately thought of Dara and Aurangzeb and wondered where they were. As far as I knew, they had not left Agra for Lahore.

It was afternoon by the time we got the whole story and it was quite a tale. As we had guessed, the messengers had come from Lahore. They had been sent by Mother's father, my grandfather Asaf Khan.

I think I'll start a new paragraph with the story of Mahabat Khan.

Mahabat Khan kidnaps the Emperor

Mahabat Khan is one of my grandfather's most trusted generals. When Father had rebelled, it was he and my uncle Pervez who had led the imperial troops and he had chased Father all across north Hindustan.

At the death of Khusro, Mahabat Khan had supported the claims of Pervez to be the heir apparent while Nur Jahan wanted Shahriyar. This led to a disagreement between the two. Mahabat was a powerful man, not afraid to challenge the Empress and he even criticized her quite openly for her ways.

You do not displease Nur Jahan and go unpunished. She hit back immediately. Mahabat's son-in-law was punished for some small mistake. He was insulted in court and imprisoned. Then the old general was ordered to march to Bengal. Instead of obeying his orders, Mahabat and his soldiers entered the Emperor's camp outside Lahore and took him prisoner.

At that time Nur Jahan and Grandfather Asaf Khan had been away from the camp and now they attacked in an attempt to rescue Grandfather Jahangir but they failed. Then Nur Jahan returned alone, gave herself up to Mahabat and joined Grandfather as a prisoner. It seems Mahabat was treating them very well but they were not allowed to move out of the camp.

As Grandfather Asaf Khan wrote, Jahangir was being allowed to live and work as he always has done but all his orders had to be first approved by Mahabat Khan. It was a truly strange situation of a man who was still the Emperor but as a puppet of his general.

The message said that for three months Mahabat has been in control of the Emperor and Empress and they had been taken from Lahore to Kabul. All this was happening last spring, exactly at the time when we were busy receiving the royal messenger in Mandu.

At least, there was some good news. My brothers, Dara and Aurangzeb, were safe in the harem in Agra.

Next Day

There is pandemonium here. Father has decided to march to the north and all of Nasik is in an uproar. The officials are bustling about getting horses and camels. The soldiers are busy packing their things, cleaning their weapons and polishing the cannons. Carts are being loaded with grain and vegetables, tents, carpets, clothes, furniture, pots and pans...

I was wondering if we have to travel with Father. We had been in Nasik only for a few months and I really did not want to travel again. I went into Mother's room and found her sitting peacefully, as a maid drew mehndi patterns on the palm of her hands.

'You are not packing, Ammi? Aren't we going too?'

Mother shook her head, 'This is a military expedition, so we stay here and wait for your Father.'

I sighed in relief and I think she guessed what I was thinking because she smiled, 'I am not feeling too well. I've told your Father, I will travel again only if we are going to Agra. If not, we stay here.'

'Oh, Ammi, I miss Agra so much!'

'I do too, sweet Jahan.' She smiled at me. 'I do too.'

A week later

Father and his army left yesterday. They were planning to move fast, so he had only a thousand horsemen with him. Shuja, Roshanara and I stood on the terrace of the haveli and watched them ride away.

The horsemen, called Ahadis, sat straight on their saddles holding tall spears that glinted in the sun. Their swords and daggers were tied at the waist of their leather jackets and they wore long, tight cotton trousers. Many had tied high, jaunty turbans that flared above their heads adding a bright touch of orange and green, blue and red to the parade. Most of them had long, curling moustaches and looked very tough and brave.

Sati-un-nissa joined us on the terrace. Roshanara turned to her, 'Sati Khanum, is Father going to rescue Grandfather from Mahabat Khan?'

'I think that is the idea.' Sati-un-nissa said absentmindedly, busy watching the soldiers.

'Mahabat Khan has a battalion of Rajput soldiers who are famous fighters.' Shuja said. 'And Father only has a thousand horses.'

'He'll lose.' Roshanara spoke worriedly. 'He always loses to Mahabat Khan.'

'Your father is going north only to find out what is happening.' Sati-un-nissa said soothingly.

'Who will help him?'

'There is your uncle Pervez. Your grandfather Asaf Khan has also not been captured and has set up his camp near Lahore. If your father is serious about rescuing the Emperor, he can always join them.'

What did she mean by the last comment? Wasn't Father 'serious' about saving Grandfather?

A week later

The house feels even emptier nowadays. Now we wait not just for news of Dara and Aurangzeb but also of Father. My brothers are still in Agra. They were then supposed to go on to Lahore to stay with the Empress but because of the trouble with Mahabat Khan they have been kept safely in the harem in the Agra Fort.

Mother was very happy and relieved to get a letter from some of the senior Mahal women saying that the boys are safe and well. Mother replied immediately, sending a letter back with the same messenger, saying that the boys are not to be sent anywhere except by the written orders of one of my grandfathers, Jahangir or Asaf Khan.

We are all scared. With Father away in the north, we are under the protection of the officials of Nasik. Father has left Chait Singh behind and he and his men guard our mansion day and night. But even then we are not really safe, so far away from Agra. Oh, I wish we were in Agra again!

Celebrations in Agra

I sit here staring out at the dripping trees and the gloomy grey-green light and dream of Agra. Our days were always so full of things happening. Then there were trips to Kashmir and Lahore, going boating on the Jamuna and picnics in the gardens of Delhi and Gulmarg.

The celebrations at the fort were the best of all. My favourites were Id and Navroz, the Persian New Year, when for a week the palaces would be lit with lamps, decorated with silk curtains and flowers. The whole city would get a clean-up, the open gutters wouldn't smell, the roads would be washed clean. During Id, in the mornings we would go to the mosque for prayers but the evenings were the time for feasts and entertainment. Singers and dancers, magicians and acrobats would come and perform.

The senior ladies of the Mahal threw their own parties and the most fabulous were those organized by Nur Jahan. One Id, she had the gardens behind the Jahangiri Mahal decorated like the heavens—silver stars and moons hung from every tree, the lamps were shaped like the sun. We were all ordered to dress in silver and gold and Mother got me loose trousers in a copper gold, a black and gold jacket and a gossamer veil embroidered all over with yellow flowers.

The guests at Nur Jahan's banquet were all the women of the Mahal and the royal men. Only the men who were born Mughal could attend these parties—my grandfather, his sons and grandsons, cousins and nephews. The only exceptions were Nur Jahan's father Itimad-ud-Daula and her brothers Asaf Khan and Mirza Khan.

The Empress always found novel ways of entertaining her guests. Once, at a Navroz feast, after the singers and dancers had gone, trays and bowls of food arrived and we saw the usual rice biryanis and pulaos. But when we took a mouthful of the rice we realized it was in fact made of sugar! The grains of rice were made of sugar and then given the colour of spices like saffron and turmeric.

As everyone exclaimed in surprise, there was much laughter and then the maids came in carrying a tray on which was a whole fish baked in spices and decorated with mint leaves.

Grandfather turned to Nur Jahan and asked, 'What is it made of, Begum?'

Nur Jahan just laughed and wouldn't say anything, so Grandfather laid a wager with her and he guessed that the fish was also made of sugar. Then he broke off a piece and took a bite and it was made of flour! Clever Nur Jahan won the wager and Grandfather gave her a pair of ruby and pearl bangles for fooling him.

A picnic at Sikandra

The biggest celebrations were on Grandfather's birthday. On that day, Grandfather would be 'weighed in gold'—this meant that he sat at one end of the giant scales and bags of gold coins would be put on the other. His weight in gold coins was then distributed among the poor in the kingdom. This practice was started by my great-grandfather Akbar.

Once, on Grandfather's birthday, we all went to Sikandra for a picnic. Badshah Akbar is buried in this marble mausoleum and around it beautiful gardens are laid out, with flower beds, shady trees, streams of flowing waters, and fountains. Grandfather has got a herd of deer living here and their dappled shadows can be seen among the trees.

Tents covered the lawns and Nur Jahan had got acrobats who performed the most amazing feats—walking on ropes on their hands and jumping through hoops of fire. Then a magician sat down on the ground and his assistants covered him with a black sheet. There was much drumming and chanting and all the while we could see the dark covered figure swaying and moving before us. Then the cloth was whipped away and the magician vanished! As we all looked around, he appeared among the courtiers, sitting happily beside the Raja of Jodhpur, who looked as surprised as us to see his new companion!

A drop of water fell on this page and smudged what I was writing and I realized I had been crying. I quickly wiped my eyes. A princess should never be seen crying.

I hate Nasik. I miss Dara and Aurangzeb. I want my room in Agra again.

News from Father
The rains have stopped and it is turning into the balmy coolness of autumn. A messenger arrived from Father this morning with the most extraordinary news. He is returning to Nasik with Mahabat Khan!

'With Mahabat Khan?' Sati-un-nissa asked in surprise. 'But isn't he in Kabul holding the Emperor captive?'

Mother looked down at the letter, 'Khurram has not given much details but it seems the Emperor is free again and Mahabat Khan decided to move southward and offer his services to Khurram.' She looked up with a frown. 'How can that be?'

The messenger who had brought the letter was waiting outside the door, across the reed screen. Mother called out to him, 'How far are they from Nasik?'

'A week's ride, Begum Sahiba,' he said very respectfully, keeping his head bent. 'They are moving slow as the Prince is not well.'

Mother sprang up and went and stood anxiously beside the screen, 'What has happened to the Prince?'

'He took ill with a high fever in Gujarat and we set up camp at Thatta as we waited for him to recover. It was there that we got the message that Mahabat Khan was coming towards us and would like to offer his services to the Prince.'

'How is he now?'

'The fever has left him, Your Highness, but there is much weakness. So he is riding in a palanquin, not on his horse. But he did write this letter to you with his own hand.'

A week later

It has been an anxious week of waiting. As Father got closer to Nasik the messengers came more frequently so we knew that he was much better but he was still too weak to ride.

What Shuja, Roshanara, I, and even Sati-un-nissa, are dying to know is the story of Mahabat Khan. My friends Bilquis and Sundari, of course, didn't even know who Mahabat Khan was and I had to tell them what a great general he was and how he had led the Mughal army to great victories. Our family history of the battling sons of Jahangir is really complicated and it took me hours to explain it to them.

'Ah! He is the man who supported Prince Pervez.' Sundari was finally sorting out our family tree.

'Then why isn't he going to Bengal and

joining Pervez there?' Bilquis wanted to know. 'It is so odd.'

She is right. It is such an odd alliance. From the day Father rebelled against the Emperor, Mahabat Khan has been his greatest problem. He led the imperial forces and often defeated Father. Why has he abandoned Pervez now and joined Father? And even more important, how did the Emperor escape from his captivity? My head is spinning with a hundred questions and nobody here has any answers.

Afternoon, the next day

Father and his men returned this morning. First we heard the drums, and ran up to the roof to look out for them.

To the rumble of drums, Father's army marched into view. In front were the Rajput soldiers riding tall horses, holding their spears and swords.

'Where's Mahabat Khan?' Bilquis was leaning so far out on the balcony she was about to fall off.

'Whose palanquin is that?' Sundari pointed.

After the horsemen, there was Father's palanquin being carried by four men and beside it rode a white-haired man who Sati-un-nissa told us was the famous Mahabat Khan.

I looked closely at one of the greatest generals of the Mughal army. A man so brave and powerful that he could even take the Emperor prisoner if he was angered. He was wearing the metal helmet of the fighter, his lined face darkened by the sun. His long curling moustache and short beard and even his eyebrows were snow white but despite his age, he sat straight on his saddle, a long sword hanging from his side. They said that he had dozens of scars from sword cuts on his body because during battles he always led his men from the front and enjoyed hand-to-hand combat with the enemy.

The soldiers rode away but Father's palanquin entered the gates of the mansion and was put down at the door. As the steward and Chait Singh hurried up, Mahabat Khan came down from his horse and then leaned down to help Father come out of the palanquin.

We all ran down to be ready to receive

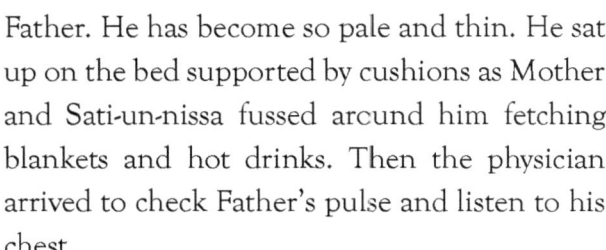

Father. He has become so pale and thin. He sat up on the bed supported by cushions as Mother and Sati-un-nissa fussed around him fetching blankets and hot drinks. Then the physician arrived to check Father's pulse and listen to his chest.

'The fever did not leave me for days, Hakim Sahib,' Father told the physician Hakim Shaukat Ali. 'Such terrible shivering and body ache. But since last week, at least, I am free from fever.'

'You had the monsoon fever, Your Highness. It is much worse in the south. Your strength needs building up.' Then the hakim went away to make his potions and powders.

The first day was spent caring for Father. He did not speak much. It was the next day that I heard the story of how Father met Mahabat Khan. It seems the Empress has triumphed again.

As we had heard from the messenger, Mahabat Khan took Jahangir and Nur Jahan to Kabul as his prisoner. He guarded them lightly and treated them with all courtesies but the Emperor could not do anything without his

permission. Nur Jahan behaved very sweetly and obediently, acting as if she had given up all hope of escape.

What Mahabat did not know was that all the while she was secretly in touch with her brother Asaf Khan. In Kabul there were two army regiments—Mahabat's troops who were Rajput soldiers, and the imperial troops called the Ahadis. The Ahadis, fiercely loyal to the Emperor, greatly resented the fact that he had been imprisoned. Then Nur Jahan sent secret letters to the generals of the Ahadis saying that Mahabat was planning to take over the imperial army and sack the generals.

Within a few weeks, the Rajputs and the Ahadis were fighting and killing each other in the streets of Kabul, and Mahabat could not control them. Realizing he would not be able to stop the fighting, he decided to return to Lahore.

On the road from Kabul to Lahore, one day Jahangir very innocently asked to review his troops. As the Emperor often does this when the troops parade before him, Mahabat did

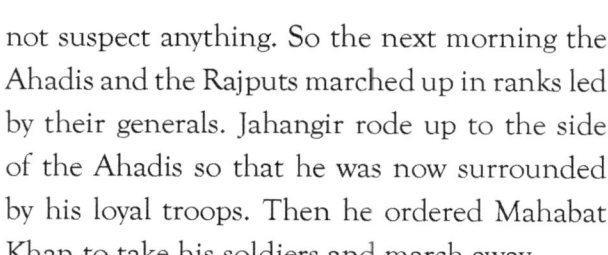

not suspect anything. So the next morning the Ahadis and the Rajputs marched up in ranks led by their generals. Jahangir rode up to the side of the Ahadis so that he was now surrounded by his loyal troops. Then he ordered Mahabat Khan to take his soldiers and march away.

Mahabat did not know what to do. If he disobeyed the Emperor and tried to capture him again, the Ahadis would fight him and he and his Rajput soldiers were badly outnumbered on the field. So he obediently marched away but instead of going to his camp he rode to the south.

Meanwhile, Jahangir and Nur Jahan, freed from the control of Mahabat Khan, rode into Lahore in triumph and once again took up the reigns of the empire. Asaf Khan and his men were waiting for them in Lahore. They were no longer in any danger. It seems the whole plan for the sudden review of the troops had come from the fertile brain of the Empress and she had succeeded in fooling Mahabat Khan.

I don't know why, but Mahabat then abandoned the cause of Prince Pervez and

decided to join my father instead. He met Father in Gujarat and Father accepted him in his army.

The next day

My head was teeming with questions, so I went looking for the one person who could explain these games of war and peace to me.

Chait Singh was guarding Father's door, he hadn't moved from there since Father came home. As Shuja and I wandered up, he looked down his straight Rajput nose and said, 'Why the glum face, Flower Begum? The Prince is back safe and sound.'

'But he has come back with Mahabat Khan!' Shuja exclaimed.

'So?' Chait Singh frowned.

'Grandfather and Mahabat are enemies...' I explained patiently, 'so now Grandfather will be angry with Father for being a friend of Mahabat Khan.'

'And the Empress will send another horrible royal order,' Shuja added.

Chait Singh sat down on a seat, made out of stone, by the door and drew us closer.

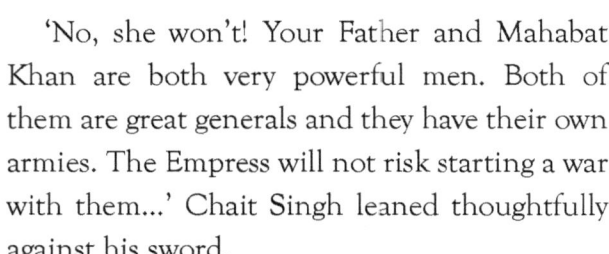

'No, she won't! Your Father and Mahabat Khan are both very powerful men. Both of them are great generals and they have their own armies. The Empress will not risk starting a war with them...' Chait Singh leaned thoughtfully against his sword.

'So we are safe here?' Shuja wanted to know.

'Yes. With Mahabat here and Prince Pervez in Bengal, the Empress has no big general to lead the imperial forces.'

'My uncle Shahriyar?' I asked, and all three of us laughed at the picture of silly Shahriyar leading the army.

Still, as I walked away, I remembered that Nur Jahan had one more card up her sleeves. My brothers Dara and Aurangzeb were in the harem of Lahore and they were the weapons she would use to keep her control over Father. Empress Nur Jahan may have lost one battle but she had not lost the war. Shahriyar could still become the next king.

The Twenty-Second Year of the Reign of His Majesty Nuruddin Jahangir Burhanpur, 1627

We are in Burhanpur

I THINK MY FATHER WAS BORN to travel because he can never stay at one place for long. During the rains and autumn we stayed in Nasik, then he got restless and now in winter we have come to stay once again at Burhanpur.

Mother and Sati-un-nissa were not pleased at having to pack and travel yet again. But as Sati-un-nissa said, it is hard to refuse Father when he is in his imperious 'I am a Mughal prince and you will listen to me' mood. You just give in and obey.

I have been in Burhanpur before. Usually it is the capital of the southern province, and only sometimes, in summer and the rains, Father shifts his capital to Mandu.

So here in Burhanpur, there is a large governor's palace inside the fort. We have more rooms, and large, well-made bathing rooms, gardens, and orchards. The palace is much nicer than the mansion in Nasik.

Nowadays, every time I travel I seem to lose some family or friends. In Mandu, it was Dara and Aurangzeb. In Nasik it was Bilquis and Sundari. Am I to spend my life travelling and losing people?

I miss them all. To fill the empty hours, I spend my days writing my memories of them. Mahjabeen Khanum had begun to teach me Persian poetry, I have carried the books here with me but I don't know who will give me lessons. She was such a patient and kind teacher. A few times she made me try writing couplets and she said that if I worked hard I could become a good poet.

I had written a short couplet and sent it to

Dara. He wants to be a poet too. Once when he said this to Sati-un-nissa she laughed and said, 'A sword in one hand and a pen in the other, hmmm...Dara? That would be just like a Mughal prince.'

It is winter

It has been some time since I wrote in my journal. Now it is the middle of winter, and Burhanpur can get cold but not as freezing as Agra or Lahore. There we used to spend our days sitting close to the warmth of the coal braziers set up in the rooms and I wouldn't have a bath for days.

I don't like Burhanpur. We had a very bad time here once. Prince Pervez and Mahabat Khan had attacked Father and he lost the battle. It was raining heavily and we had to retreat from Burhanpur with the imperial troops chasing us. Mother was ill and we had to get on horses and ride in the mud and rain.

It was a miserable time. There was little food, most of our luggage had to be left behind and we lived in dripping tents. When we crossed

a swollen river the boats kept filling up with water. And all the while we heard of the imperial troops getting closer and closer. I really thought we would all die.

Burhanpur

Let me describe Burhanpur and compare it with Agra. It is a small town with narrow lanes that are often just bare earth and very dusty. Open gutters run alongside the lanes and they smell. The houses are small, single storeyed, each with a courtyard inside. There are few open spaces or parks.

In comparison, Agra has broad roads often paved with stones over which the horses' hooves and carriage wheels move with a loud clatter. The lanes wind in and out like serpents and there are mansions and bazaars on both sides. At night, the shops are all lit with earthen lamps and large torches burn in the corner of the lanes.

I love the bazaars of Agra. I have seen them through the curtains of the palanquin as we have gone past. These rows of shops sell everything from clothes and jewellery to pots and pans.

The shopkeepers sit inside on mattresses laid on the floor, serving their customers who arrive in palanquins and horse carriages.

In the corners are flower shops with garlands swaying in the breeze and baskets of flowers stacked outside. There is always a crowd at the paan shops where the betel leaves are filled with spices and sweet fragrances. Like Mother and Sati-un-nissa, I too like chewing paan and I love the way my breath becomes fragrant with the smell of cardamom and the essence of roses.

Harem women go shopping

At times, the Mahal ladies decide to go shopping. On one occasion, I remember, there was much excitement in the palaces with everyone dressing up and putting their money in bags. The slaves and maids bustled about getting palanquins and calling soldiers to escort them.

The soldiers would ride off first to the main bazaar and they made all the people leave so that the Mahal women could shop without being seen. Then, the palanquins arrived and the women in their colourful veils floated out

like a bunch of excited butterflies. Chattering and excited, they ran around the bazaar where the shopkeepers stood by the doors of their shops bowing and welcoming them in.

The best jewellery shops are in the Durr-e-Baha Bazaar and Mother and Sati-un-nissa always headed for them. At Mother's favourite jewellery shop, the shopkeeper would get his wife and daughter to serve Mother so that she could shop at ease. I remember the last time we went to that shop, the shopkeeper's wife welcomed us in and we sat down on the mattress on the floor that was covered with a fresh white sheet. We leaned against the bolsters sipping pomegranate juice as the women carried in boxes of jewellery and, opening them, laid them out before us.

There were trays of rings, a necklace of emeralds gleamed against the black velvet, a pair of bangles set with turquoise was in the shape of peacocks. Mother picked up a thick bangle in gold made like a filigree of lace, set with tiny rubies and spots of glittering diamonds. She

held out her arm and the woman slid the bangle over her hand.

Mother also bought a pair of studs shaped like roses for my ears and Roshanara chose anklets in silver that tinkled sweetly when she walked. Sati-un-nissa, who has a passion for rings, bought three of them, the prettiest was shaped like a leaf and it covered half her ring finger. She wears it often here in Burhanpur.

Later

I forgot to write about my uncle Pervez. He had died in autumn in Bengal. He was thirty-eight years old and probably died of drinking too much. At least that is what Mother and Sati-un-nissa said.

Hearing the news of his death, Roshanara said, 'So now there are only Father and Shahriyar left.'

Mother who was playing checkers with Sati-un-nissa stopped rattling the dice and said, 'What is that supposed to mean, Roshan?'

'That Father and Uncle Shahriyar will now

fight for the throne. And with the Empress supporting Shahriyar, can we bet on Father?'

'Aren't you clever, my little Mughal princess?' Mother said sarcastically. 'Have you had your bath yet or do you plan to spend the morning telling us your thoughts about war and peace?'

'I am sure your father would love to hear what you have to say,' Sati-un-nissa added.

Roshanara just grinned and drifted out of the room. If Mother had spoken to me like that I would have wept for days but nothing ever affects my sister.

Roshanara had said something that was true. Father had his own spies in the court of the Emperor. They had sent reports from Agra saying that Grandfather was quite ill. He found it very difficult to breathe, and he felt cold and feverish all the time in winter, even when they had braziers lit in his room.

The kingdom is being run entirely by Nur Jahan. She dictates all the order and Jahangir only puts his signature over the royal seal. Sometimes, he is too ill to even read what he is signing. All those years of drinking and opium have really ruined his health.

Nur Jahan is being helped in the work by her brother, my grandfather Asaf Khan. He had stayed loyal to the Emperor even during the years when my father Shah Jahan, his own son-in-law, had been in rebellion. So this brother-sister team, who were not Mughal, are now running Hindustan.

Once Jahangir fell ill, I think Father had hoped that he would be summoned to Agra to help Nur Jahan but that did not happen. He still waits impatiently in Burhanpur while she treats Shahriyar as the crown prince and Asaf Khan watches everything and stays silent.

We sit here in boring Burhanpur. My two brothers lost and alone in the harem in Agra, my father lives a life of uncertainty and it is all because of Grandfather.

I hate my grandfather. I really do...I hate the great Emperor Nuruddin Jahangir.

As I was writing the last sentence I did not hear Sati-un-nissa creep up from behind me. She read what I had written and said softly, 'Do

you really hate him, Jahan? He is not such a bad man, you know.'

Dreaming of Agra again

All day I have been thinking about what Sati-un-nissa said. Do I really hate my grandfather?

All my memories of him are such happy ones. His smiling face at the family gatherings, the way he would tease Mother about her love for jewellery. How he loved to lay wagers with the Empress about everything and when he lost he would give her these marvellous gifts. He is a kind man.

Once, on Dara's birthday, he and I went to Grandfather's room early in the morning to pay our respects. Dara was carrying a small gift for him—a painting he had done of a flowering rose bush. He knew Grandfather liked paintings.

When Grandfather's steward took us in, he was busy listening to some reports being read out to him by his officers. So we sat down in a corner and watched him work. He would listen to the report and then dictate his orders to the writer sitting near him.

Once the officials had bowed and left Grandfather called us closer. Dara bowed low and touched his forehead and said, 'I came to offer my greetings to Your Majesty. Today is my seventh birthday.'

'Of course!' He looked delighted. 'How could I forget that, Huzoor Dara Shikoh?' He kissed Dara on the forehead, blessed him with a long life and said, 'Seven years old? *Kya baat hai!* You are becoming a man now and will soon lead the army like your father.' He clapped and his steward came to stand by the door and Grandfather said, 'Bring Prince Dara's birthday gift.'

In a moment the steward returned carrying something covered by a cloth on a large tray. Grandfather whipped off the cloth with a flourish and we stared at a silver birdcage, inside was an eagle that turned its head to stare at us with its huge, golden eyes.

'Oh, Grandfather!' Dara was so delighted, he could hardly speak. 'H...ho...how did you know I wanted an eagle?'

'Ah ha! Don't you know I am the Emperor

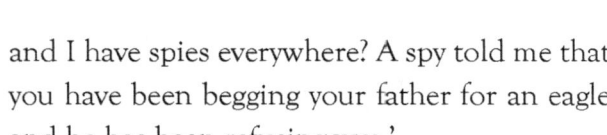

and I have spies everywhere? A spy told me that you have been begging your father for an eagle and he has been refusing you.'

'Father told you?' I asked.

He shook his head. 'A spy told me. I cannot reveal names.'

I think Mother may have mentioned Dara wanting an eagle to Nur Jahan.

Dara stood admiring the eagle. It had yellow feathers flecked with black and its claws had sharp, pointed nails. One leg was shackled to the stand in the birdcage with a small silver chain. As we stared at him, he stared back just as calmly, the curved beak turned haughtily up towards us.

'What will you call him?' Grandfather asked.

Dara thought for a while and then said, 'He is Kataar. Because his claws are sharp as daggers.'

'Shaabash!' Grandfather laughed. 'That is an excellent name. Worthy of a Mughal.'

Then Dara took out his small painting and said, 'I have a gift for you, too.'

'For me?' Grandfather's eyebrows rose up and he looked very pleased. 'How wonderful!'

He opened the packet and looked at Dara's painting. I have to admit, it wasn't really very good. The roses drooped on the branches and looked wilted and the leaves were a strange shade of brown-green because Dara had mixed up the colours. But listening to Grandfather's praise you would have thought that Dara had painted a masterpiece. He put the painting on a table beside him saying he had to show it to the Empress.

A few days later, Dara and I were summoned once again to Grandfather's room. It seems he was going to visit his painters and wanted us to come with him.

Grandfather loves miniature paintings and employs many artists. They all work at the painter's atelier called the Musawwir Khana—the house of the painters. Grandfather visits them often and even tells them what he wants them to draw. Whenever he travels he takes some of his painters with him and makes them do drawings of the land and the animals and birds.

Dara and I had wanted to see the Musawwir

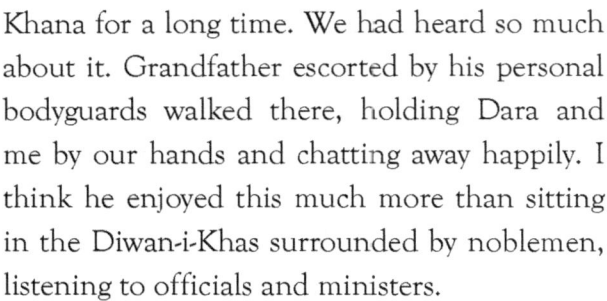

Khana for a long time. We had heard so much about it. Grandfather escorted by his personal bodyguards walked there, holding Dara and me by our hands and chatting away happily. I think he enjoyed this much more than sitting in the Diwan-i-Khas surrounded by noblemen, listening to officials and ministers.

The painters all worked in a large, airy room in a corner of the fort. As we entered, they all stood up to bow and Grandfather waved to them to go back to work. The painters sat on cushions on the floor. Sheets of paper were spread on low tables before them on which they created their paintings.

One artist named Hafeez was about to begin a painting and Dara and I sat down beside him to watch him work. He took a rectangle of thick, creamy paper; one side of it had been painted a flat white. Now he rubbed the back of the sheet with an even stone so that the white paint became smooth and shiny.

Over the white paint he carefully began to draw the lines of the drawing. He was going to paint the portrait of a woman and now he

drew the profile with a pointed stylus. Once the outline of the drawing was complete he would fill in the colours that he mixed in small seashells.

Some painters were working with colours— reds and greens, blues and yellows, dipping their brushes into the seashells lying beside their tables. Miniature paintings are small, usually the size of books, so very fine brushes are used to colour them. When painting the finest lines like the eyebrows or the pattern on a veil, they use brushes that have just a single strand of rabbit hair.

All the while, Grandfather was sitting on a low seat studying the paintings that had been recently completed by the artists. A drawing of a dancing peacock was criticized because he felt the colours were not right. Then he liked one of a turkey and gave the painter a gold mohur as a reward. But I liked the picture of the dancing girl the best.

Burhanpur in spring

Father has not travelled for some months now and his health is improving slowly. Since the

time he rebelled against Grandfather five years ago and went into exile, he has been constantly on the move, fighting battles. Some he has won, others he lost and all the while he has struggled to keep his army together. It has not been easy. The doctor says that all these years of physical and mental strain are finally taking their toll.

Even this time when he went towards north after the rebellion of Mahabat Khan, bad luck dogged his steps. First, the Rajput general Raja Bhim Singh fell ill and died. Then all the Raja's personal horsemen abandoned Father's army and decided to go back to Rajasthan. So Father was left with just half his men and then at Thatta in Gujarat he himself fell ill with the fever.

As Chait Singh says, if Mahabat Khan had attacked Father instead of joining him, then Father would have been in real danger. Father's fortunes seem to be changing.

Messages come occasionally from the north. Grandfather Jahangir is very ill and he is only happy in the clear air of Kashmir where he can breathe more easily. So the Empress has taken

him there. My brothers are in Lahore where some of the ladies of the harem are staying in the fort palaces. Father sent a request that now that he has been forgiven by Grandfather he be allowed to return to Agra or the boys be sent back. But the Empress refused both the requests.

It has been one whole year since I saw them last. They must have grown so much taller. I am thirteen now, so Dara is twelve and Aurangzeb, nine. Mother says I have to start behaving like a lady now and not run around the fort like a washerwoman's daughter. When Father heard this, he laughed and said that I was the prettiest washer girl he had ever seen.

The Empress obviously still distrusts Father and wants Shahriyar to be the next king. That could be soon enough if Grandfather Jahangir stays so ill. I look at Father's thin face, the hollowed cheeks and shadowed eyes and fear for him. What will he do if the Empress succeeds in her plans for Shahriyar?

I never understood why Father lost her trust because he had always been careful not to

displease her. Sati-un-nissa says it was because Grandfather Jahangir was becoming more dependent on Father, and the Empress did not like it.

His years of exile were filled with disappointments. Many of the men he depended on the most have been disloyal to him. Even his closest adviser Abdur Rahim Khan-i-Khanan's loyalty wavered once, when he nearly deserted Father.

This was the time when Father had lost a battle at Burhanpur and we had to retreat by crossing the swollen river. Abdur Rahim wrote to Pervez offering him his services and this letter fell into Father's hands and he was deeply hurt.

When Father confronted Abdur Rahim with the letter, the old man said that he regretted writing it and he had done so in a moment of weakness. He said he did not really want to desert Father like a traitor. Then Father brought him into the harem to meet Mother and made him swear that he was going to be like a brother to her and would never betray her.

Such an act was very rare, where a man who

did not belong to the family should be allowed into the harem to meet a princess. This is called *Mahram Sakht* meaning 'one who could enter the harem'. I have heard that during the reign of Badshah Akbar, his friend Raja Birbal was made a *Mahram Sakht*. It is a great honour and one that Abdur Rahim wouldn't easily forget.

Still Father cannot really trust people. If an old family friend like Abdur Rahim can plan to betray him, anyone can.

It is still spring

But I am not enjoying this! The long days just don't pass! Burhanpur is not beautiful like Mandu. I do enjoy the roses in the palace garden though and picked up a bunch to put beside Father's bed.

We all wait for the messenger to bring news of the north. It is a great help that my grandfather Asaf Khan is still in the court with Jahangir because he sends all the news to Father.

Father often reads out his letters to us and we heard of how Jahangir can no longer walk

without help. The Empress is always beside him. All the best doctors of the kingdom are in attendance but no one can really help him.

Even now, writes Grandfather Asaf Khan, the Emperor has not forgiven Father. He refuses to read the letters that Father writes to him. He is so angry that from the time Father went into exile, his name is no longer mentioned in the royal memoirs of Grandfather Jahangir.

When he was well, Grandfather used to dictate his memoirs with details of his daily life, his travels, the events of the time, the work of the court, news of the Empire, and even what he saw and experienced. He ordered that Father was no longer to be mentioned by name in the book but was to be called 'bi-daulat'–the Wretch. Even today when the royal history is being written by others, that is the hurtful name given to Father.

'I feel sorry for him,' Mother said one day to Father. 'Khusro and Pervez are dead. He cannot forgive you. All he has now is Shahriyar.'

Father sighed, 'Shahriyar as king! I find it hard to imagine it and I don't think the empire

will survive such a calamity. Shahriyar has never led an army, he has never fought a war, and he knows nothing about running an empire. He has spent his days going hunting and visiting dancing girls. He will lose everything that was built by my grandfather Akbar.'

'The Empress will rule through him.'

'She cannot lead a military expedition or meet the officials or ambassadors. She cannot tour the empire inspecting the land. She is a woman.'

'And one day she will die. Then what will Shahriyar do?'

This is all we talk about in Burhanpur. What will happen when Grandfather Jahangir dies? What will the Empress do? And we all wonder in our hearts, what will Father do.

Another Jumma

Being a Friday, we all went to say our prayers at the local mosque. It is a very old mosque, a simple stone-and-brick building that needs repair. After getting off his horse, before entering the mosque, Father suddenly stopped

and began to look around. We stood right under
the main entrance. He looked up, studying the
stone arch and then he thoughtfully walked
around the door and corridors inside.

After the prayers, Father once again
wandered around studying the mosque, its
prayer courtyard, the minarets and domes. The
chief priest, the Imam, came up to Father and
followed us.

Then Father turned to him and asked, 'Imam
Sahib, how long has it been since this mosque
was repaired?'

'Many years, Your Highness. We have no
money for repair and the outer walls and gates
are falling down. I only try to keep the mosque
going.'

'Would you let me repair your mosque?'

The Imam was so surprised and delighted he
nearly tripped and fell as he bowed and bowed
again, 'Huzoor, if you could save this mosque, it
would be like a blessing from Allah!'

'I'll come again tomorrow with my builders,'
said Father.

As we walked away, the Imam was still

bowing to Father and his white bearded face was wreathed in a smile.

Father is happiest when he is building something. He loves nothing more than sitting with rolls of drawings of buildings and talking to the craftsmen who carve on the marble and set them with coloured stones. While at Agra, he would wander about the palaces of Agra making plans about how he would change them.

Now, everyday he sits with carvers and architects, brooding over designs of pillars and arches, patterns for carvings and layouts of the garden. He plans to cover the domes of the mosque in marble and have minarets set in a pattern in black and white. He loves to use marble in his buildings.

Sometimes he draws the designs himself. Last evening, he was sitting at his table, drawing flowering lilies and floating clouds that he wanted carved on the pillars. Roshanara and I were watching him.

'Where did you learn to draw, Abbu?' Roshanara asked.

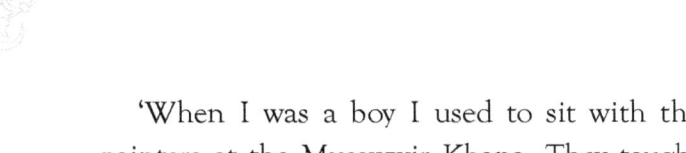

'When I was a boy I used to sit with the painters at the Musawwir Khana. They taught me to draw.'

'Grandfather Jahangir once took Dara and me there,' I said. 'He really loves paintings, doesn't he?'

'Yes, he does.' Father smiled. 'I used to go there with my grandfather Akbar. He liked paintings but he enjoyed designing buildings more. I am like him.'

I remembered Mother once telling me of how Father and Badshah Akbar were very close to each other. Father was his favourite grandchild and he often travelled with him, going hunting or on military expeditions. Father even sat at gatherings of nobles when he was only a small boy.

'He built such beautiful palaces at Fatehpur Sikri,' Father said, musing. 'He taught me how to plan a city and build palaces and gateways.'

'He also built the Agra Fort, didn't he?'

'Yes. He liked to use red sandstone. I like to use marble.'

Visiting the new mosque

The work of repairing the mosque went on very fast. It began in early spring and now it is summer and it is almost complete.

I think working on that mosque was the best medicine for Father. He is once again his quick, energetic self. Father hates being idle and there is very little for him to do in Burhanpur.

Today we are all to go and see the completed mosque. Best of all, we are going on elephants and not in palanquins. I love riding elephants!

The next day

Oh, yesterday was such fun! We were all so excited. Roshanara, Shuja, Murad and I were ready early in the morning. Three elephants were waiting for us at the door, with the howdahs on their backs. The animals had been painted with colourful patterns on their trunks and ears. The mahouts stood by their heads. Mother and Sati-un-nissa were to travel in a closed howdah; we were going in an open one.

I looked up at Father's favourite elephant and said, 'Hello, Zabardast! How are you?' and

I gave him some apples and bananas. Zabardast carefully picked up the fruits from my palm with his soft trunk and put them in his mouth. Then he flapped his huge fan-like ears and swayed his head, making the bells at his neck ring. I think he understood me. Elephants are very intelligent animals.

When we were ready to go, the mahout climbed up to sit at the elephant's head. He did it so easily. As the elephant bent one knee he held on to its ear and climbed up. Then he tapped the elephant and it knelt down for us. Small wooden steps were put next to the animal and we clambered up to sit in the howdah.

As the elephant stood up, suddenly we were high above the ground, sitting on its broad bony back. Then as it began to move, we swayed from side to side at every step and the bells hanging from its neck went 'cling clang' keeping a beat to its steps. Father is so used to travelling on elephants that he can lie down in the howdah and go to sleep. He says the swaying makes him sleep better.

The mosque is gleaming with white marble

domes and black and white minarets. The gateways now have carved walls and the prayer courtyard is paved with granite. After the prayers, the Imam came and bowed to Father.

'Your Highness,' the old man said, 'will you permit me to say something?'

'Of course.'

'You have many fears and worries in your mind about the future. Let me assure you, all your wishes will come true.'

'My last days have not been easy.'

'I know, but the dark days are receding, my Prince. The path is not easy but you will succeed.'

As we walked away, I noticed that Father was smiling to himself. Maybe Burhanpur is not such a bad place after all.

News from Nasik

Today a messenger arrived with a letter from Sundari for me.

Sundari is getting married. She is thirteen, like me, and has been betrothed since she was seven. Her marriage is in autumn and she has

invited me to go to Nasik. I wish I could go but I know Father would never allow that.

Bilquis is also to be married next year. I wonder if I will ever marry. Many of the Mughal princesses never do because the princes do not like the idea. Married princesses mean sons-in-law who could also claim the throne. There are so many unmarried princesses in the Mahal. Unless Mother can find me a prince in another royal family in some other kingdom, I will have to share their fate.

Banarasi arrives

I should introduce Banarasi properly. He is such an interesting person. Dara and I had a name for him. We called him the jester-messenger.

Banarasi is a messenger, one of the fastest in the kingdom. His work is to carry messages from the royal court to the provinces. Sometimes he uses horses, at other times, he runs.

On the main roads of the kingdom, Badshah Akbar built many inns and these inns have stables. So Banarasi changes horses at these inns, rests and eats and moves on

again. But when the message has to be taken to some remote place, like an army camp in some faraway province and there are no inns or horses, Banarasi just runs.

Nowadays, Banarasi is employed by Grandfather Asaf Khan and is often in Burhanpur with messages from him. Whenever he comes I run to be close by to listen to him because not only does he bring the messages, he is also full of the latest news from the Emperor's court and all the interesting gossip and rumours.

This morning Banarasi arrived again. The Emperor was in Kashmir and Grandfather Asaf Khan who was with him had sent the message. So Banarasi had travelled from Kashmir to Burhanpur and it had taken him a month to do so. After giving the bundle of letters to Father he went off to rest and eat.

It was evening when Father called him for a chat. He met him in the verandah outside Mother's room so that she could also hear him. Sitting beside Mother, I could see Father with Banarasi, across the reed curtain. Father sat on a low seat and Banarasi was perched at his feet.

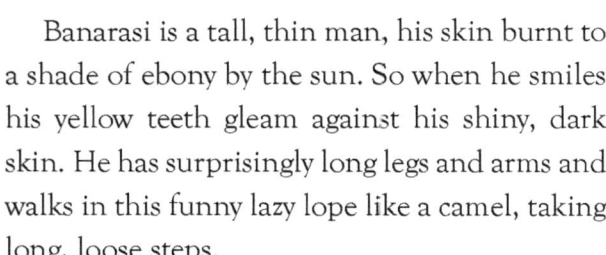

Banarasi is a tall, thin man, his skin burnt to a shade of ebony by the sun. So when he smiles his yellow teeth gleam against his shiny, dark skin. He has surprisingly long legs and arms and walks in this funny lazy lope like a camel, taking long, loose steps.

I think he has a really funny face, with a flattish nose and two round eyes that he rolls about when he talks. He chatters all the time he is awake and his eyebrows dance about, his hands fly in the air and listening to him, you have to laugh. I think all those days of travelling alone makes him talk so much.

'You have eaten and rested, my friend?' Father asked.

'*Ji, Huzoor.* Your steward treats me with great care. I have eaten enough for two men.'

'How is my father, His Majesty Jahangir?'

'Not well, Huzoor.' Banarasi's face fell with sadness. 'Not well at all. He has become very thin, his face is grey with pain and he has completely lost his appetite, even wine does not tempt him. Taking a few steps makes him pant heavily and he has to be carried everywhere in a chair.'

Father leaned forward anxiously, 'Can't the physicians do anything?'

Banarasi shook his head. 'All the best hakims and vaids of the kingdom are in attendance. They even got an English doctor to come from Surat. Sometimes a new medicine revives him for a while but the effect does not last long.'

Father was silent for a long while and then said softly, 'I wish I could be beside him now. I know he needs me.'

'It would have been so good if Huzoor were near His Majesty. You could help him but the Empress and Prince Shahriyar...' Banarasi stopped and shook his head mournfully.

'I know. She will never let my father call me back to the royal court.'

Banarasi shrugged, 'And all this for Prince Shahriyar. He does not deserve to be king.' Then he grinned, his yellow teeth gleaming. 'If the great Emperor dies we could get a bald king in his place.'

'What?' Father asked puzzled.

'Oh, of course! Huzoor does not know! You

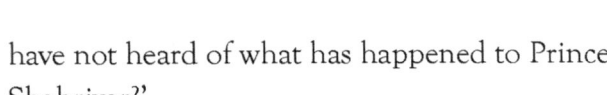

have not heard of what has happened to Prince Shahriyar?'

'What?' Father said again.

'He has a mysterious disease of the skin that has made him lose all his hair.' Banarasi was clearly enjoying the tale he was telling.

'No hair?' Father looked astonished. 'None at all?'

'None at all, Huzoor. No hair on his head, no beard, not even eyebrows or eyelashes...'

'I can't believe this!' Father began to laugh. 'Banarasi, you are not making this up to amuse me, are you?'

'No, Huzoor!' Banarasi rolled his eyes as his face was split by a huge grin. 'You know me. I may exaggerate a little but I do not lie. Prince Shahriyar is as bald as an egg. The disease attacked him in Kashmir. The physicians said that the cold weather has made it worse. So he has now gone to stay in Lahore.'

'And has the hair appeared again?' Father was still smiling.

'No, Huzoor. He dreams of a moustache

every night but is disappointed when he looks in the mirror in the morning.'

At this comment Mother laughed out so loudly that hearing her, Banarasi's grin widened. He had enjoyed making a princess laugh.

Once Banarasi left, Mother turned to Sati-un-nissa. 'I am trying to imagine a bald Emperor Shahriyar sitting on the throne in the Diwan-i-Aam. The throne of Akbar and Jahangir.'

I can't imagine it either. That throne is for a prince like my father. He is the best among Jahangir's sons and he deserves to be the king. Why won't the Empress understand that?

Autumn in Burhanpur

The grey monsoon skies are gone and the sky is dotted with fluffy white clouds that look like balls of cotton. I lie on the terrace and watch them, seeing mountains and serpents, dragon faces and flying birds.

Time moves so slowly. There is little news from the north except that Grandfather Jahangir and Nur Jahan are still in Kashmir.

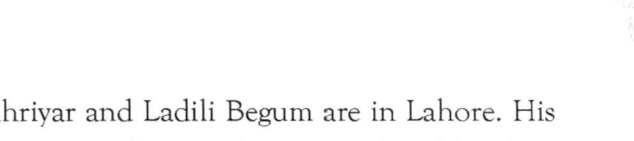

Shahriyar and Ladili Begum are in Lahore. His skin ailment has not been cured and his hair has not returned!

My brothers are in Kashmir with the Emperor's harem. They are doing their studies and go for riding and archery lessons. It is more than a year since we saw them. Already their faces are becoming hazy in my mind and if I don't see them soon I'll forget what they look like. I try hard to remember them clearly but their faces keep moving away as if hidden by a mist. I miss Dara so much.

I miss them all. Dara, Aurangzeb, Bilquis, Sundari and Mahjabeen Khanum. Even Grandfather Jahangir. I wonder if I will ever see him again.

News from the north

Banarasi arrived this morning. My grandfather, Emperor Nuruddin Jahangir is dead.

We are in mourning. When Father heard the news, he sat still as a stone and then held his head in his hands and wept. Prayers are being said for his soul at the mosque. Father said his

prayers and then called his advisers and officers to the court room.

I do not know what is going to happen now but the following days will not be easy. I know that. Mother sits staring out of the window or is at her prayers. I have never seen her pray so much before.

Will there be war? And my brothers so far away... Oh, please Allah, keep Father safe. Keep my brothers safe. Please...I am so afraid for all of them.

Next day

Father left for the north this morning. He has all his officers and horsemen with him. His army is being led by Mahabat Khan.

In the morning, the army gathered for departure and the Imam of the Burhanpur Mosque came to say prayers and bless them. He tied an amulet on Father's arm; the taweez would protect him from the swords of his enemies.

As we stood and watched them ride away, I realized that I was happy to see the old general

Mahabat Khan ride behind Father. Once I feared him, now I pray that he protects Father.

How Grandfather Died

Grandfather Jahangir had spent the summer and the monsoons in Kashmir but by the end of autumn it was becoming too cold there. So he and the Empress decided to move south again to Lahore. But the journey was too much for his weakened body and he died a fortnight's journey away from Lahore.

My grandfather Asaf Khan was there when the Emperor died and he moved quickly. First, he sent Banarasi with an urgent message that Father should gather his army and move as fast as he could to Agra. The royal treasury was at Agra and it was the capital of the Empire. So Father had to capture both before Shahriyar could do so.

Banarasi had never travelled so fast in his life. He covered the distance from Kashmir to Burhanpur in just twenty days!

Father and his men chose to travel on the fastest horses and now they are racing to the

north. Chait Singh, who has stayed behind to escort us, says Father could get to Agra in a fortnight. We are all packed and ready to follow him. We begin our journey tomorrow.

On the road to Agra

We are on the move all day but travel slowly. We are travelling in horse carriages and bullock carts. The entire family, baggage, the maids, servants, cooks, guards, soldiers, washermen and their families are with us. Everyone wants to go to Agra with us.

Father and his troops have moved far ahead but the messengers come nearly everyday. Grandfather Asaf Khan's messengers also reach Father regularly from Lahore. So we know what is happening at the royal courts of Lahore and Agra.

Grandfather Asaf Khan moved quickly after the Emperor died. He sent his soldiers to the royal camp so that Nur Jahan was surrounded. She stays beside Grandfather Jahangir's body but she cannot move out on her own or do anything without her brother's permission. The soldiers are all loyal to Asaf Khan and after years of being quiet and obedient, my grandfather has finally taken the reins in his hands.

Things would have been difficult if Prince Shahriyar and his wife Ladili Begum were beside her. Because then she would have immediately declared him king and the soldiers and officers would have found it hard to refuse to give him their loyalty, but Shahriyar was in Lahore and Nur Jahan found herself alone.

Grandfather also moved swiftly to take away my brothers from the control of the Empress. Dara and Aurangzeb are now staying with him in Lahore and are safe. When the message arrived about my brothers, Mother fell on her knees and prayed in gratitude, and later, all day she couldn't stop smiling.

'Why was Mother so worried?' Roshanara asked Sati-un-nissa curiously. 'My brothers were in no real danger, were they?'

'The Empress would have never harmed them,' I added. 'Would she?'

'True. She would never harm them. But at a time like this when a king dies, with princes

fighting for the throne, there is much confusion among the people around the king.'

Both Roshanara and I must have looked very puzzled because she then explained further.

'The people in the court always try to please the powerful. At such a time, some fool of a nobleman, some harem woman or a slave could think Nur Jahan and Shahriyar would be pleased if Shah Jahan's sons did not live. Nur Jahan would never harm any of you but someone holding a grudge against your parents could.'

Roshanara was silent for a while and then she turned to me and her voice quavered, as she finally understood the danger our brothers faced, 'Oh Jahan! They could have been poisoned! Like Uncle Khusro.'

'Yes,' said Sati-un-nissa quietly. 'It is not always a Mughal who does the deed but they always get the blame.'

I knew what she was talking about. I wondered if Uncle Khusro had been poisoned by someone trying to please Father. Did Father know?

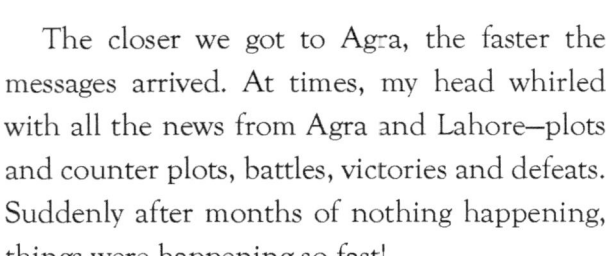

The closer we got to Agra, the faster the messages arrived. At times, my head whirled with all the news from Agra and Lahore—plots and counter plots, battles, victories and defeats. Suddenly after months of nothing happening, things were happening so fast!

In the royal camp, on the way to Lahore with Jahangir's body, Grandfather Asaf Khan had a problem. As the king was dead, another Mughal prince had to be declared the new king very quickly. But Father was still far away from Agra and was not there beside him.

If Grandfather delayed any longer, there was the danger that Shahriyar would get the news of the Emperor's death and would immediately claim the throne and have prayers said in the mosque in his name. Then the imperial troops and the noblemen would support him against Father. So Grandfather came up with a clever trick.

My uncle Khusro had a son named Dawar Baksh. Grandfather got him to the royal camp and had him declared king with all the proper ceremonies. The plan was that in this

way Shahriyar would be kept away from the throne and the moment father arrived, he and Grandfather would take away the crown from Dawar Baksh and Father would become king.

In this way the imperial troops would stay loyal to Dawar Baksh and Asaf Khan and not shift their loyalties to Shahriyar. In a fight for the throne, it was very important to keep the imperial troops on your side.

When I heard this news, it took me a while to understand it because I couldn't even remember ever having seen Dawar Baksh.

I frowned and asked Mother, 'When Father takes over the throne, what will happen to Dawar Baksh?'

'He will probably be imprisoned,' she replied calmly.

'Or killed? Poisoned like his Father?' I asked.

'Who knows? It is his fate.' Mother shrugged indifferently.

The Empress strikes back

Nur Jahan was surrounded by troops loyal to Asaf Khan as she travelled towards Lahore with

Jahangir's body. She was guarded and watched night and day and even then, she somehow managed to send a message to Shahriyar giving him the news of the death of Jahangir and ordering him to put together an army to fight Asaf Khan. No one knows how she managed to do this.

Shahriyar rushed around collecting arms and soldiers and once he had an army, he moved out of Lahore to claim the throne. The armies of Asaf Khan and Shahriyar met outside Lahore and Shahriyar was defeated. That was to be expected. He had never led an army before and his men were ill prepared and inexperienced while the imperial forces are the best fighters in the kingdom.

It looks like this time Empress Nur Jahan lost the battle. Once he realized that he could not win, Shahriyar ran away and hid in the harem in the fort at Lahore. He was dragged out from there, blinded and imprisoned in the dungeons of Lahore Fort. Dawar Baksh, poor puppet of Asaf Khan, rules as king. My grandfather Jahangir lies in state in Lahore, receiving the

homage of the people. He will be buried there and not in Agra.

We got news that Father is already in Ajmer, a few days' ride from Agra. Here he met his friend Raja Karan Singh of Mewar once more. It was Karan Singh who had given us sanctuary in his lake palace in Udaipur when Father was in trouble. Now, he is the first to meet Father and pay his respects. Father has presented him with many honours and his younger brother Arjun Singh is now travelling with Father with his regiment of Rajput soldiers.

The messenger further describes how Father is proceeding down the road to Agra at the head of a big, ever-growing army, and the people who stand on both sides are hailing him as the king and showering flowers. The noblemen and chieftains are offering him their respects and then joining his army with their men.

The First Year of the Reign of His Majesty Emperor Shahabuddin Muhammad Shah Jahan
Agra, 1628

We are in Agra

AT LAST! I AM BACK IN AGRA!

We arrived yesterday morning and Roshanara and I were so excited we forgot to behave like princesses and had the curtain of our palanquin open so that we could see everything. I wasn't going to miss anything and fortunately, Mother and Sati-un-nissa were in their own palanquins and could not see us.

We entered Agra in a gorgeous parade. First there were twelve horsemen, followed by the three palanquins and then the horse carriages, bullock carts, elephants and camels. All moving down the road lined with people welcoming us back with shouts of joy.

It felt wonderful! We had left Agra in such disgrace and now such a wonderful homecoming.

Our cavalcade moved slowly down the road to Agra Fort and the people showered us with flowers all the way. Once in a while, I stuck my head out to feel the flower petals fall on my face like a soft, fragrant rain.

Roshanara and I laughed with happiness as we went through the main gateway of the Fort and then moving past the outer palaces we entered the Mahal area. Father received us at the door to the Mahal.

As the palki bearers laid down the palanquins, he hurried out to welcome Mother. A crowd of Mahal women had gathered and there was much excitement and laughter, as holding her by the hand, Father led Mother into her new apartments.

This palace is the best in the Mahal. Once Nur Jahan had lived here and now Mother, as

the new Empress of Hindustan, is going to stay
there.

We followed Father as he showed us around.
I realized the palace had been newly furnished
with shimmering silk carpets on the floor, the
low seats were made of silver, set with gems
and with velvet cushions. The doorways had
swaying curtains of pearls. There were large,
carved wooden chests for our things and in the
niches in the walls there were silver perfume
sprays and incense holders, jewel boxes and
trays of fruits. The bolsters scattered over the
carpets were covered in silk and velvet and
everywhere there were garlands and bouquets
of flowers. After years of staying in army
camps and old musty forts, this was like being
in heaven!

Mother's eyes were glittering with happiness
as she turned to Father with a laugh, 'Oh
Khurram! This is a palace made in paradise!'

He smiled at her. 'It is what you deserve,
Arjamand. This is the palace of the Empress of
Hindustan, Begum Mumtaz Mahal.'

We all stared at him in surprise.

'From now on you are Mumtaz Mahal, beloved queen of Shah Jahan.'

Mother is very pleased with her new title. Now Father who was first named Khurram is Emperor Shah Jahan and Mother who was born Arjamand Bano Begum is Mumtaz Mahal.

I remain Princess Jahanara. Thank Allah. I like my name and I don't want any fancy titles.

Three days later

The days have gone by in such a whirl that my head spins. Roshanara and I have spent our days getting dressed in new clothes and going with Mother to visit the senior Mahal ladies.

Among those we met were some of Grandfather Jahangir's wives, who were in mourning for him. Then there were two of Father's older wives, Akbarabadi Mahal and Fatehpuri Mahal, and also his eldest daughter Purhunar Begum. She was born before Father married Mother and she is the only child he has had from any other wife except Mother.

Mother is very careful about paying her respects to the senior queens. She may be

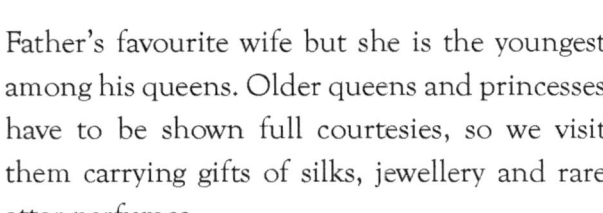

Father's favourite wife but she is the youngest among his queens. Older queens and princesses have to be shown full courtesies, so we visit them carrying gifts of silks, jewellery and rare attar perfumes.

Mother, Sati-un-nissa, Roshanara and I walked through the Mahal to the palace shared by Akbarabadi Mahal and Fatehpuri Mahal. All the way Mother was instructing us on how to behave.

'Bow to them and say salaam...do not forget to ask of their health...do not talk unless spoken to...eat slowly and don't ask for more...'

'Oh Ammi!' I protested. 'We know what to do. We have gone visiting before.'

'That was six years ago. You two have been running wild since then. Things are more formal in the Mahal.'

'You are in trouble, Jahan,' Sati-un-nissa grinned at me. 'No more exploring of forts and hide-and-seek in the gardens with your brothers.'

'I am going to explore. Try and stop me.' I said stubbornly. 'I have forgotten what this fort

looks like, so I am going to wander. I have to see all the palaces once again.'

'Why haven't you gone wandering yet?' she teased. 'Worried you will get lost?'

'I am waiting for Dara.'

Meeting the queens

Akbarabadi Mahal and Fatehpuri Mahal were waiting for us in their living room. Roshanara and I behaved perfectly, making Sati-un-nissa give us a small, curved smile. As Mother made polite conversation with the queens, we sat behind the women munching walnuts and almonds and sipping glasses of apple juice.

Both the begums are older than Mother and treat her with a cool courtesy. They said a polite thank you for the gifts she gave them but did not bother to open the packets. I don't think they like her much.

Can you blame them for that? Once Father married Mother, he forgot about them and only visits them out of courtesy. They may be wives of the Emperor and live in the lap of luxury but they are still forgotten women.

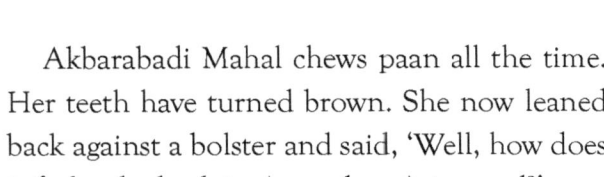

Akbarabadi Mahal chews paan all the time. Her teeth have turned brown. She now leaned back against a bolster and said, 'Well, how does it feel to be back in Agra, dear Arjamand?'

Mother, who is always a little subdued before them, smiled, 'It feels wonderful to be back in the Mahal once again, Your Highness. And to be able to meet you after all these years.'

Fatehpuri Mahal, who is kinder, nodded. 'Six years in the wilderness. It must have been difficult for you.'

'At times I nearly gave up hope of ever seeing my family again. When Khurram fell ill and the boys were far away in Lahore, I thought we had been cursed and our days of misfortune would never end.'

'I hear you are living in Nur Jahan's palace now,' Akbarabadi Mahal said with a slight, crooked smile. 'All newly furnished in silks and velvets.'

Mother nodded silently.

'Where is Empress Nur Jahan now?'

'In Lahore. She has chosen to stay there as our revered Emperor Jahangir, god rest his soul,

has been buried there. I hear she plans to stay near his grave and build a mausoleum over it. She told my father that she would like to be buried near the Emperor when she dies.'

'Well, she can hardly come back to the Mahal!'

'My aunt will always be welcome here.'

'You may say so Arjamand, you are a kind woman, but Khurram would never have Nur Jahan creating trouble in Agra.'

Again Mother remained silent.

As we were leaving, Fatehpuri Mahal walked with us to the door. There she turned to Mother and said, 'I am happy for you, Arjamand. I think Khurram deserves the throne and you have been a very loyal wife. But were these deaths necessary? Prince Daniyal's sons, too?'

Mother's eyes were cold, her face stiff with anger. 'I am just a wife, Fatehpuri Begum. No one asks my permission in the affairs of men. Why don't you ask Khurram about this?'

'I will.' Fatehpuri Mahal was turning away. 'And that poor boy Dawar Baksh!'

On our way back, Mother looked so angry

I did not have the courage to ask her any questions but I have to find out what happened to Dawar Baksh. Why did Fatehpuri Mahal say deaths? Who else has died?

That night

Oh joy! Oh wonderful wonderful world!! Tomorrow I'll see Dara again. And Aurangzeb and Grandfather Asaf Khan...

I am so excited I can hardly sleep!

Next Day

I stood back and studied my brothers. Both have grown taller, especially Dara. They came rushing into the palace very early in the morning followed by Grandfather Asaf Khan. In a moment all of us were creating a lot of noise, hugging and kissing and tumbling about.

I looked closely at Dara's face and said, 'Are you getting a moustache yet? You are nearly thirteen now, dear Prince.'

He grinned and peered into my face. 'Have you got one? You're nearly fourteen, sweet Princess.'

Aurangzeb drifted up to me with a shy smile.

'You've grown fatter, Aurangzeb!' I laughed. 'No more coughs and colds?'

He shook his head. 'I have learnt to ride, Jahan Apa, and to fence and do archery.'

I gave him a quick hug. 'You are the bravest and cleverest of my brothers.'

'Riding, fencing, archery...' Roshanara grinned. 'You two have been enjoying yourselves.'

'Hardly,' Dara said glumly. 'There were lessons every day. Mathematics and Grammar, Persian and Geography. The Empress was very strict with us.'

'How is she?' I asked curiously. 'Did you meet her after Grandfather died?'

'We went to say goodbye,' Dara said. 'She has become very thin and quiet. She visits Grandfather's grave every day and spends her days in prayers.'

'I hear Mother's got a new title?' Dara asked.

'She is Begum Mumtaz Mahal, the Queen of the Palaces.' Roshanara grinned. 'And do you know Father's full title?'

'Shah Jahan, King of the World?' Aurangzeb guessed.

'Oh no! He is no longer Prince Khurram or just Prince Shah Jahan. He is Emperor Shahabuddin Muhammad Sahib Qiran Sani Shah Jahan!'

'That's impressive!' Aurangzeb's eyes were huge with wonder. 'He sounds like the king of the universe!' And we all had a fit of giggles.

'When is the coronation?' Dara asked.

'Next week, and we have to get new clothes!' said Roshanara.

We go wandering

The five of us—Dara, Shuja, Aurangzeb, Roshanara and I were dying to see the Agra Fort again. We all had vague memories of it and Aurangzeb did not remember it at all. We heard it was being specially decorated and we wanted to see everything.

After a whole day of begging, Mother agreed to let us go but with conditions. Chait Singh and a maid would go with us. We had to see the fort very early in the morning before the gates

were opened to people. And we had to stay within the walls of the fort.

We began our walk on an early winter morning, it was still misty and cold and we were all wrapped up in our warm quilted jackets. We walked past the red sandstone palaces of the Mahal with their open courtyards surrounded by the rooms where the women stayed. It was very quiet, most of the women were still asleep and only the maids and slaves were stirring.

As we walked through the beautifully laid out gardens with the flower beds, lawns, fountains and lotus pools and along the stone pathways, Dara asked Chait Singh, 'Where will Father be crowned?'

'In the Diwan-i-Aam. That is the largest hall in the fort. All the noblemen will attend the ceremony so it will get very crowded. Want to see the place?'

'Yes!' we all said together.

The Hall of Public Audience, the Diwan-i-Aam is where the king meets his subjects. Everyday he sits and listens to petitions from people and passes judgement in the trials. It is a domed

hall with rows of carved pillars inside. At one end is a decorated alcove up a few steps and on this platform the throne is kept. I remember Grandfather Jahangir sitting on the low silver, gem-encrusted seat, leaning against bolsters and my grandfather Asaf Khan as a senior minister, standing before him, handing him the notes from the people gathered in the hall below.

The hall was being cleaned and decorated for Father's coronation. All the things of the workmen were piled in the corners. The men would have left the fort at nightfall because no one except the royal family and their personal servants and guards are allowed to stay there at night. They would come into the fort early morning and begin their work.

'Where next?' Chait Singh asked. 'Diwan-i-Khas?'

'Yes!' we all said once again.

The Hall of Private Audience, the Diwan-i-Khas is a smaller hall where the Emperor sits with his important officials. He receives the ambassadors of other kingdoms and listens to reports from governors and generals. I like this audience hall with the slim pillars and curving arches. Shuja and Aurangzeb ran up and down the empty hall calling to each other.

My favourite part of the fort is the private palace of the Emperor called the Khas Mahal. This is where Dara and I came to see Grandfather Jahangir that morning when Dara gave him the painting. They are, by far, the most beautiful rooms in the fort.

Every inch of the stone walls is carved with flowers, vines, fruits and geometric patterns. Some walls are painted in pretty designs of dancing peacocks, flowering trees and herds of running deer. The floors are covered with a pile of silk carpets so thick and soft your feet sink in them and the colours of the carpets glow in the rays of sunlight. Enamelled lamps hang from the ceiling, and tall standing lamps are placed in the corners beside incense holders.

I noticed Father had changed the furniture and the carpets. In his bedroom, his swords, shields, daggers and spears stood on a table in the corner. The next room was where he got ready, and his clothes, shoes and jewellery were

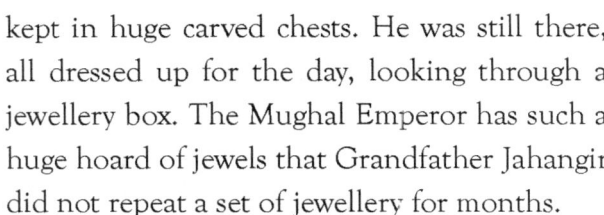

kept in huge carved chests. He was still there,
all dressed up for the day, looking through a
jewellery box. The Mughal Emperor has such a
huge hoard of jewels that Grandfather Jahangir
did not repeat a set of jewellery for months.

Father was slipping on rings, a triple string of
pearls and his steward tied two jewelled armlets
above his elbows. He looked up to see our
grinning faces at the door.

'What are you all doing out so early?' Then
he saw our escort and said, 'Oh good, Chait
Singh is with you.'

Chait Singh salaamed Father. 'They have
been bothering the Begum Sahiba saying they
want to see the palaces.'

I wandered out to the balcony of the Khas
Mahal. Below was the slowly moving, brown
waters of the Jamuna. A faint mist was rising
from its waters as the first rays of the sun fell
on the ripples, touching them with gold. What
could be more beautiful than a balcony over the
river? I breathed in happiness.

I could hear my brothers and sister chattering
in the room behind me, with Father's deep

voice rising above them. Somewhere a bird sang
and I could hear the crunch of the footsteps of
marching soldiers as the guards were changed at
the gates. I am home.

Meeting Fatehpuri Mahal

In the afternoon, the boys had gone off to
practice archery. Roshanara was taking a
nap. Mother was sitting with half a dozen
seamstresses who were making her dress for the
coronation. Sati-un-nissa had gone off to meet
her old Mahal friends and I had nothing to do.

I wandered about the Mahal as my memories
of the place came back. The gardens and
courtyards, the baths and open balconies where
the women sat to enjoy the breeze. It was after
lunch, most of the women were in their rooms
and it was quiet. Maids wandered about carrying
clothes and linen, pots and pans to be washed
at the wells.

In one corner of the Mahal is a small
mosque that is only used by the Mahal women.
I wandered into the silent prayer courtyard; I
love mosques, they are such peaceful places.

Even when they are empty, the sound of prayers seems to float in the air. Close to the mihrab, the arched recess in the wall that faces towards Mecca, I saw a bowing figure of a woman saying her prayers. I did not want to disturb her, so I leaned against a pillar, dreaming in the warm sun.

The woman completed her prayers and turned and I saw that it was Fatehpuri Mahal. As I stood up and greeted her, she saw me and smiled. 'Child, what are you doing in the mosque? You should be busy preparing for the coronation celebrations tomorrow.'

'My clothes are all ready and I like this place.'

'You like saying your prayers?' I nodded. 'That is good,' she said.

She came and sat down beside me. Her dark, kohled eyes were bright and kind. I have always been a little afraid of Father's other senior wife, the paan-chewing Akbarabadi Mahal. She has a sharp, bitter tongue and says things aimed to hurt you. Fatehpuri Mahal is a kinder and gentler person.

She looked around the empty courtyard and

said, 'One day, I would like to build a mosque.' She laughed. 'Now that Khurram has become Shahenshah, maybe he'll give me the money for it.'

'I would like to design a mosque too,' I said dreamily. 'With domes covered in a zigzag pattern in black and white marble.'

'You should come and visit me sometimes, Jahan. I think you and I can talk of many things. Also, I hear you love books. I have a nice library, especially of Sufi poetry that you will like.'

'I'd love to! Can I also bring Dara?'

'Of course! Come anytime. I am just an idle woman, my days are filled with unimportant things.'

We stayed silent for a while, soaking in the warmth of the sun. It was nice, the way we sat so comfortably, like old friends. It is only with your old friends that you can be peacefully quiet together. I liked her and could talk to her so freely, the way I can talk to Sati-un-nissa. She somehow seems to understand.

Why is it that I can never talk to Mother like this? To her I am just a daughter, someone

to be dressed in pretty clothes and ordered to behave and then forgotten. She looks bored if I try to talk to her about anything important. For her it is her husband and her sons who are important. She would not have wept so wildly if Roshanara and I had been sent as hostages to Nur Jahan instead of Dara and Aurangzeb. She would have sighed and moaned for a few days and then gone back to caring for Father and my brothers, worrying about her hair and skin and buying new jewellery. I have never understood it, she was a daughter too.

'Begum Sahiba,' I broke the silence, 'can I ask you something?'

'Of course, child. If I know the answer.' She spoke in a sleepy manner, eyes closed, her face raised to the sun.

'What happened to Prince Dawar Baksh?'

That woke her up. She sat up straight and turned to look at me.

'I remember everyone said Father had Uncle Khusro poisoned. And Dawar Baksh is his son.'

'That was just gossip.'

'And this time?'

She sighed. 'You are a Mughal, I suppose it is time for you to know how this family is run.' She paused and then spoke slowly as if she was choosing her words carefully. 'There were four executions that took place before your father arrived in Agra. Poor young Dawar Baksh, two sons of the late Prince Daniyal, and Shahriyar. All of them were killed. Shahriyar had been blinded first in Lahore.'

'Who was Prince Daniyal?'

'He was Jahangir's younger brother and died many years ago.'

'And Father ordered that they should all be killed?'

'Yes.' Her single word seemed to echo all around me.

I swallowed. There were more things I needed to know.

'I can understand about Shahriyar, he was against Father but the others did not challenge him for the throne. Did they?'

'They could do so in the future. Their greatest fault was that they were male, they were Mughal...' she sighed. 'You see the Mughals have

no law saying that the eldest son will become king. Any male member of the family can claim the throne. So if you are a Mughal you either become king or you die. If you are lucky you get blinded or imprisoned.'

'I don't always like being a Mughal.'

She smiled. 'Neither do I.'

As Fatehpuri Mahal got up to go, she smiled down at me. 'Visit me sometime, sweet Jahan. You and I have to plan our mosques.'

I thought of Father and Mother in the past few days. Busy and happy planning the coronation ceremonies. Father meeting noblemen in the Diwan-i-Khas; Mother receiving their wives in the Mahal. Both of them wandering about ordering the maids and servants. Did either of them visit the Princess Begum who was Khusro's wife and Dawar Baksh's mother? And I thought of Ladili Begum who was Mother's cousin and Nur Jahan who was her aunt, sitting by the graves of their dead husbands in Lahore.

I really don't like being a Mughal.

The Coronation of the Emperor of Hindustan Shahenshah Shahabuddin Muhammad Sahib Qiran Sani Shah Jahan Agra, 24 January 1628

My father is now king

ON FATHER'S CORONATION DAY, we all wore our new clothes. The seamstresses had been working night and day to complete them on time. I had seen them, bent over their stitching late into the nights, working by candlelight.

I had got a silk angrakha jacket over light churidaar pyjamas in a dark blue, embroidered all over in silver. Over it, I wore the dupatta in gauzy silver. Roshanara's costume was a similar design but in a bright yellow and gold. Sati-un-nissa was looking very stylish in purple and gold peshwaz jacket over loose pyjamas and the boys were all wearing gold jackets over red pyjamas with coloured sashes tied at the waist.

Sati-un-nissa opened the jewel boxes and gave necklaces and bangles, earrings and anklets to Roshanara and me. The boys got pearl necklaces, armlets, bracelets and rings. Sati-un-nissa herself was wearing dangling earrings made with strings of pearls set with small sapphires. The earrings were so long they lay across her shoulders and her necklace was made up of diamonds and amber set in design, like flower petals of gold. Roshanara, the vain little thing, picked up a thumb ring with a mirror set in it, so that she could admire her own face in it.

Mother had been getting ready for hours and now she came out and we all gasped when we saw her. I have never seen her look so majestic and dazzlingly beautiful.

She wore a deep red peshwaz jacket up to her knees over tight trousers. Over this she

wore a loose, transparent gold coat open in front and floating around her. The peshwaz was embroidered in gold thread set with hundreds of tiny pearls. The dupatta that she had thrown overhead was red and so heavy with gold embroidery that it kept slipping off her shoulders.

Roshanara and I went closer to admire her jewellery. She wore a string of pearls with a gold pendant in the parting of her hair. Her heavy earrings set with diamonds dangled to her shoulders. Around her neck was a double string choker of pearls and two long necklaces set with diamonds, rubies and emeralds. Her arms were covered with gold and pearl bangles halfway up to her elbow and she wore rings set with gems. When she walked her heavy gold anklets jangled at every step.

She had darkened her eyes with kohl and reddened her lips and cheeks with lac and Sati-un-nissa must have sprayed her with a whole flask of attar because the room smelled of her jasmine perfume.

She stood framed by the door and asked, 'How do I look?'

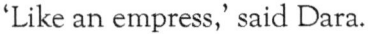

'Like an empress,' said Dara.

We all walked through the covered passages to the section of the Diwan-i-Aam that had been screened off for the Mahal women. Many of the women were already sitting there and I saw Fatehpuri Mahal among them and she smiled when she saw me.

I sat down next to the reed screen so that I could see the hall outside. The Diwan-i-Aam was packed with all the biggest noblemen, the amirs and omrah of the kingdom, all dressed in silks and jewels. The scene was like a painting of dazzling colours. Rich carpets, velvet hangings on the pillars, gold railings and filled with the men preening about like peacocks.

I looked about trying to spot the men I knew. There was Grandfather Asaf Khan looking very gorgeous in a white and gold peshwaz with a red shawl thrown over his shoulders. There was Mahabat Khan with his upturned white moustache and Abdur Rahim Khan-i-Khanan talking to Arjun Singh, the young prince of Mewar. My brothers stood on the side of the throne with Chait Singh. Even my baby brother

Murad was among them, looking around wide-eyed.

Then I heard the drums and knew that Father was about to arrive. A hush fell in the hall as everyone turned to stand facing the throne. Then the master of ceremonies came to the door and in a loud, echoing voice announced Father with all his many titles.

Roshanara, who had parted the reeds of the curtain to get a better view, turned to me with a wicked smile and whispered, 'I never knew Father had so many titles!'

I whispered back, 'Do you think he can remember all of them?'

Sati-un-nissa was smiling as she hushed us to keep quiet.

Father entered and walked up to sit on the throne. He seemed to glitter in gold, silver and jewels. His peshwaz was gold silk embroidered with pearls and silver thread. He wore the best Mughal jewels. First the diamond and emerald sarpech—the ornament that held two flaring feathers in place on his turban. Around his neck was a six-string pearl necklace with pearls

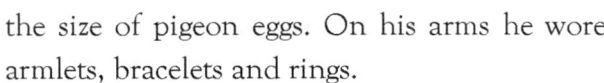

the size of pigeon eggs. On his arms he wore
armlets, bracelets and rings.

A dagger with a jewelled hilt called phool
katara was thrust through the kamarbandh,
the silk belt that he wore around his waist. His
shoes with pointed front were embroidered in
silver and set with pearls and turquoise. Two
men stood behind him waving murchhals, yak-
hair fans, and a row of them stood to the side
bearing the emblems of royalty—the gold and
silver disks shaped like the sun and moon set
on top of wooden poles. The throne was a silver
seat with carved legs set with gems and with a
silk canopy above it with a fringe of pearls.

As Father sat there on the throne, leaning
against a bolster, his sharp, fair profile etched
against the dark red silk canopy, he looked so
handsome my heart missed a beat. This was a
real king.

The coronation ceremony is simple. The
royal priests, the imams, prayed and blessed
him. Then the nobles came forward one by one
to greet him and give their royal gifts. There
were trays of gold mohur, jewelled boxes, rare

diamonds, pearls, bolts of precious silks from China, perfumes from Europe and many kinds of jewellery. The amirs and omrah knew that Father loved jewellery.

Then Father made his first announcements as a king. He told the gathering of Mother's new title of Mumtaz Mahal and that she was to receive a yearly allowance of ten lakh rupees. He said that Begum Nur Jahan would receive a pension of two lakh rupees every year. Grandfather Asaf Khan was now the Vazir, Father's prime minister and he was presented with a royal dress. Mahabat Khan was made the landlord of the jagir of Ajmer. Prince Arjun Singh of Mewar was given gold mohurs, jewels and horses.

The reward that pleased us the most was when faithful Chait Singh marched up to Father to receive a jagir in the Punjab and a bag full of gold mohurs. Our friend Chait Singh was now a nobleman in the Mughal court!

Then the master of ceremonies announced that celebrations will go on for a month. There will be feasts and fireworks, singing and dancing, magic shows, acrobatics, elephant fights, wrestling, horse races and polo. The people of Agra will have a long holiday. They will be given food and clothes from the palace. The palaces, bazaars, mosques and the walls of the city will be decorated with lamps at night.

Good night

It is past midnight as I sit writing the last page of my journal. My eyes are heavy with sleep, my fingers ache a little, and the candle is spluttering and dying. It has been a very long journey since I began writing this journal in faraway Mandu and today was a very long day.

Life has become very busy, there is so much to do. Mother as the head of the harem needs my help. She is still not well and Sati-un-nissa has to take care of her. Also, now that my life is so much quieter, I have a wish to write some poetry...

I, Jahanara, Mughal Princess, bid you good night.

The Real Jahanara in History

JAHANARA'S CAREFREE DAYS AS A pampered Mughal princess ended quite soon. When she was seventeen, her mother Mumtaz Mahal died at childbirth. Jahanara now became responsible for her four brothers—Dara, Shuja, Aurangzeb and Murad—and two sisters Roshanara and Gauharara who was a baby. She was also made the head of the harem. Fortunately loyal Sati-un-nissa was always at her side.

Shah Jahan was heartbroken at the death of his beloved wife. He built the beautiful marble mausoleum, the Taj Mahal over her grave. Later, two of his other queens Akbarabadi Mahal and Fatehpuri Mahal and Mumtaz's companion

Sati-un-nissa Khanum were also buried in the outer courtyard of the Taj.

Shah Jahan's reign was the most magnificent of the Mughals. His court was legendary for its riches and grandeur. He sat on the jewel-encrusted Peacock Throne and he owned the famous diamond, the Kohinoor. He also built a new capital city in Delhi that he called Shahjahanabad. In this new city, the main bazaar was called Chandni Chowk, the Silver Street, and it was planned by Jahanara.

Jahanara as the head of the harem was given the title of Padshah Begum. It was a position of great responsibility, as she had to manage a huge establishment of women. She was also a trusted adviser of her father.

Neither Jahanara nor Roshanara ever married but she organized the weddings of all her brothers and her youngest sister Gauharara. There are miniature paintings of the wedding of Dara, showing gorgeous processions and feasts.

Jahanara was closest to her brother Dara Shikoh and they shared an interest in literature and philosophy. She herself became a good

poet and wrote a book about the Sufi saints of the country. Surprisingly, she was also a good businesswoman, managing the running of the port of Surat that Shah Jahan had gifted to her and trading with the West with her own fleet of ships.

Over the years, her brothers grew apart and the greatest animosity was between Dara and Aurangzeb. Dara, his father's favourite, stayed in the capital while the other three were sent off on military expeditions and as governors of provinces. Among them, Aurangzeb became the most efficient governor and a good general.

Jahanara's life took a tragic turn in 1658 when Shah Jahan fell ill. Thinking he was dying, his sons marched out to claim the throne. Jahanara favoured Dara while Roshanara supported Aurangzeb. Though Dara had the imperial forces, he had little experience in fighting and he lost to Aurangzeb.

Dara was captured, paraded in chains through the streets of Delhi and then executed. Murad was first imprisoned and then executed. Shuja and his family, running away from Aurangzeb's

forces, vanished in Bengal and were probably killed by river pirates. Jahanara pleaded for mercy for her brothers but she failed to change Aurangzeb's mind.

Aurangzeb imprisoned his father in the Agra Fort and took the throne of Delhi. Jahanara refused to live in the harem in Delhi and went to Agra to care for Shah Jahan. The heartbroken Emperor lived for eight years, spending his days looking out of his balcony at the Taj Mahal. When he died he was buried there, beside his wife.

At Shah Jahan's death, Aurangzeb went to Agra and personally escorted Jahanara back to Delhi. He gave her a palace to live in and once again made her the head of the harem. This did not please Roshanara who had been the senior-most princess till then. In spite of the fact that Jahanara had supported Dara and not him, Aurangzeb remained very close to her and visited her often.

Both Jahanara and Fatehpuri Mahal built their mosques. Jahanara's mosque is in Agra and Fatehpuri Mahal's at one end of Delhi's

Chandni Chowk. The Agra mosque has domes with a zigzag pattern in black and white marble.

Jahanara died in 1681 at the age of sixty-seven. She is buried in the courtyard of the shrine of her favourite Sufi saint, Sheikh Nizamuddin Auliya in Delhi. At her request, her grave is a simple enclosure open to the sky and the top of her grave has only bare earth on which plants and grasses grow. A panel at the head of the grave is inscribed with a poem written by her.

> *Let naught cover my grave, save the green grass*
> *For grass well suffices as a covering,*
> *For the grave of the lowly.*

Jahanara, gentle Mughal princess, loving sister, poet, thinker and businesswoman, lived with courage and grace and has never been forgotten.

www.ingramcontent.com/pod-product-compliance
Lightning Source LLC
Chambersburg PA
CBHW051107030726
47504CB00006B/1834